BEW...
WE...

The screen lit up, giving a view of the slowly turning gas giant. Suddenly the intruder seemed to leap forward, to show an irregular artificial shape clearly outlined against the brilliant hues of the planet's dense atmosphere.

"That's a Klingon cruiser, Jim," McCoy declared.

"I can see that, Bones," Kirk muttered. "Mr. Sulu, sound red alert. Mr. Arex, align phasers to . . ."

"Receiving transmission from the Klingon ship, Captain," Uhura interrupted.

"Acknowledge their signal, Lieutenant."

The Klingon who appeared on the viewscreen was seated in his counterpart of Kirk's command chair. His attitude was one of relaxed attention. Except for the tight set of his lips, he appeared almost friendly.

And when the image had fully resolved at both ends of the transmission, he even smiled . . .

THAT COULD ONLY MEAN ONE THING . . . TROUBLE!

STAR TREK
LOG SEVEN

Allan Dean Foster

Based on the Popular Animated Series Created
by Gene Roddenberry

BALLANTINE BOOKS • NEW YORK

Library of Congress Catalog Card Number: 74-8477

ISBN 0-345-24965-8-150

Manufactured in the United States of America

First Edition: June, 1976

Cover art supplied by Filmation Associates

For all the fans of Star Trek,
everywhere . . . ignore the ignorant
and stick to your phasers!

STAR TREK LOG SEVEN

Log of the Starship *Enterprise*

Stardates 5536.3—5536.9 Inclusive

James T. Kirk, Capt., USSC, FS, ret.

Commanding

transcribed by
Alan Dean Foster

At the Galactic Historical Archives
on S. Monicus I
stardated 6111.5

For the Curator: JLR

THE
COUNTER-CLOCK
INCIDENT

(Adapted from a script by John Culver)

I

A warm light seemed to suffuse April's face as he stared at the drawings. Soft, caressing, intense—the kind of gentle radiance Rembrandt used to edge his portraits with.

The works hanging on the wall before him, which had inspired such a reverent gaze, would never hang in any museum, would never raise the brow of the lowliest art critic. Yet April's mind applied a critic's terminology to them. Masterpieces—exquisite, sensuous, drawn with unsurpassed skill and vivid realization—they were.

True, the drawings had no depth beyond the minimally necessary. There was no attempt to give body to the colossal conception so skeletally sketched. The use of color was minimal, every drawing done in unrelieved blue on white.

But that didn't matter. His mind filled in the myriad colors that would be added later.

"Magnificent, isn't she?" the old man standing on April's left murmured. "Even in the preliminary blueprints. The soundness of Franz Joseph's original design holds up well. You know, there was a time when people thought he designed these ships only for amusement, that they'd never have any practical application."

"Hard to believe," April agreed. "Still, they were well ahead of their time." He peered harder at the wall full of drawings. "NCC-1701, Class One ... that's a heavy cruiser, right?"

"Sure is," Commodore van Anling admitted. "Her major components are being put together out in the San Francisco yards right now. I could take you out there, but"—he nodded toward the wall—"there's much more to be seen in those prints than in a few irregular

3

masses of metal and plastic. Free-space assembly won't begin for another eight months yet."

"I see." April turned to the smaller, deceptively frail-looking man. "But why tell me all this, sir? Why call me away from my regular duties?" The light in his eyes deepened to an expectant gleam. "Am I going to be assigned to her?"

The commodore nodded, unable to suppress a slight smile.

April's voice rose like a small boy's. "What section, sir? If you have any idea, if it wouldn't be against regulations to tell me . . . !"

"I do and it isn't," van Anling told him, moving to a chair facing the wall.

"Engineering?" April prompted.

"No."

"Communications, then? Surely communications." The commodore shook his head. "Sciences . . . a security post?"

"No . . . no." Under the pencil-thin white mustache the older officer cracked an irrepressible grin.

"For heaven's sake, sir, give me to the Klingons, send me up for disobedience . . . but *tell* me! I've got to restudy whatever section it is, got to prepare. . . ."

"You sure do," van Anling informed him somberly, "because you're going to be in all of them." At April's blank stare, he added, "Because she's going to be your ship . . . *Captain* April."

"My . . . ship?"

"You're going to be her captain . . . her first captain," the commodore continued. April eyed him uncertainly, but there was no tag to the incredible pronouncement. Therefore it had to be true.

Slowly April turned, to stare anew at the wall filled with diagrams and blueprints. His gaze traveled from one to another, but all at once the regular lines seemed wavy, the precision gone. Lines clashed crazily, ran blindly into adjoining ones. The gleam in his eyes was gone, replaced suddenly by signs of another emotion.

Fear. Fear and a thrill so overwhelming he felt as though the combination would shove his heart right out through his chest. All of a sudden Robert April was the happiest man in the world . . . and he was scared to death.

"I . . . I'm not ready for this, sir," he finally managed to confess.

"That's all right," van Anling replied benignly. "You've got a whole year to make yourself ready. Better get to it, son."

In the harsh, gray shadows of the moon, beneath hills of devastated ash and pumice, an unlimited-range, high-resolution navigational computer finished digesting a gigantic body of minutiae. The results of many days of intense electronic cogitation were regurgitated in the form of a tiny printout on an insignificant little shard of tape.

The tape was carefully routed from the computer processor through an intermediary to the person in charge of the installation, who then relayed it to the captain of the small vessel resting in orbit high above the station. The captain passed it on, together with the requisite orders, to his own navigator. That worthy conferred with his two associates—one mechanical, the other only partly so.

The thing, he explained, would have to be aligned so and so at a speed of such and such, to achieve the optimum eventual impact. From time to time the ship's gunnery officer nodded knowingly or added a comment or correction of his own. Eventually everyone agreed. The results of the discussion were transmitted to the captain, who gave his approval and issued the formal order, which the gunnery officer executed.

Although the projector mounted on the small ship looked unimpressive, its efficiency was astounding. There was no flash, no concussive aftershock, no rumbling boom, of course, but the projector did its job nonetheless. Sensors immediately took over, announcing unemotionally that the projectile was on course at the proper speed. It would reach its target in approximately two weeks, four days, sixteen hours and assorted minutes.

The captain of the small ship eyed the tiny blip until it had faded completely from the sensitive tracking screen. More than anything else, he wished he could be there when the projectile impacted on its target. Destiny, however, had ordered more mundane activities for him on that distant day. He sighed. If he were lucky, they might be able to pick up the results on the tracking monitors—if they were still in the area.

Construction of the battle cruiser was proceeding smoothly. More smoothly, in fact, than had the construction of any similar vessel in some time. Possibly the Vulcan foreman had something to do with it. But whether through causes superhuman or supernatural, it began to be whispered among the construction crew and Starfleet personnel that this was going to be an especially blessed ship, a lucky ship. . . .

The projectile possessed no power units of its own. It had no sensing equipment, no detectors, no screens—nothing that could be sensed by any type of sophisticated energy-detection equipment. There was nothing to spoil the eventual surprise of its arrival, and it had to be perfectly aligned when fired. Divergence of even a hundredth of a degree could cause it to miss its intended target entirely. So its planners, both electronic and human, had been careful. It held to its course and flew silently on its way.

The United Federation of Planets Starfleet assembly station swung in majestic orbit around Earth. It resembled a bombed toy factory.

Gigantic preassembled sections of ships were boosted to this spot from half a hundred points on Earth's surface; special components from as many more deep-space cargo containers were unloaded. Thousands of elements were manufactured nearby, in dozens of enormous drifting factories, their production facilitated by zero gravity and total vacuum. Each of several million parts had to fit into sisters and brothers within a thousandth of a millimeter. Humanoid minds had conceived the project, but none of it would have been possible without the aid of machines.

One section was devoted to assembling two massive warp-drive engines. Construction crews working in triple shifts seamed the yawning sections together, work continuing around the clock.

An unusual pause in the work rhythm accompanied the placing of shielding from Tashkent. Assembly totally halted as the second-shift engineer-in-charge slowly turned his flexible armored worksuit to face the glowing Earth below. He arranged his suit carefully, moving the upper part in a particular way. His motions were directed toward a distant point on the planet's surface. They were as accurate as he could make them without benefit of detailed instrumentation. A slight divergence would not matter. His thoughts exceeded the actual movements in importance.

He quickly resumed directing the shielding installation. Below, Mecca had rotated past, turning majestically with the rest of the world.

In bits and pieces the huge ship began to form, sections of a white puzzle taking shape against a chill black background. Each crew, each shift, prided itself on being more accurate than its predecessor. Every coterie of seamers drifted on tethers and tried to outdo its counterparts for smoothness of joining and accuracy of component integration. The technicians and constructors and fabricators who set the lanes for the ship's bowling alley in place did their job with no less care and finesse than did the cybernetics crew responsible for locking the central computer into the ganglion of electronic nerves which stretched the length and breadth of the steadily maturing ship.

While construction proceeded with remarkable speed and efficiency, a tiny projectile continued toward a preselected point in space.

Eventually the day came when no more massive boosters lifted from the Earth's surface. No components required a last recheck; every bit of instrumentation had been certified operational. Everything was in place, from photon torpedos to potted philodendrons.

Several thousand strong, the construction crews began to assemble around the finished ship. Individuals in worksuits drifted in, as did crews of two or three manning engineering lighters—several hundred looking on from the orbital assembly stations that boxed in the construction area. All looked on as the first crew finally took official possession of their ship.

The engineering staff alone did not proceed at once to assigned quarters. Starship engineers seldom used their on-board personal cabins. They lived in jeffries tubes and cramped accessways and in the free spaces between computer housings.

April barely had time to check out the glistening chronometer in his quarters. Luxuriating in the comparative spaciousness of the captain's cabin would have to wait. He had a ship to command.

It was a short turbolift ride to the bridge. His first-shift officers awaited him there. Slowly, appraisingly, he looked them over one at a time. Were they all as nervous as he was, he wondered? Some had had more time in Starfleet than he did, albeit in noncommand ratings. Did any of them feel the same overpowering mix of fear and exultation, terror and expectancy, that had been building in him since that day the commodore had shown him this ship, at the time only a smattering of diagrams spread on a wall outside the San Francisco naval yard?

To April's relief, it was First Officer Shundresh who smoothly broke the silence.

"Ready to get under way, Captain."

"Very well, Mr. Shundresh. All stations stand by."

Suddenly his fear was gone, replaced by a strange calmness. It all seemed so natural somehow, as if he had been doing this for years. Walking forward, he assumed his position in the command chair. His body melted easily into the deceptively blunt contours. The chair was comforting beyond imagination, in a way that bordered on the erotic.

Leaning over, April pressed the proper button and spoke with a reassurance that sprang from just-tapped regions. "Engineering?"

"Chief Engineer Kursley," the thick voice filtered back. "Standing by for orders, sir."

"Activate warp-drive engines, Chief."

"Activating warp-drive, Captain." Kursley turned to the prime engineering board. She eyed her subordinates, then muttered a silent liturgy. It might have been a prayer, might have been something else. She engaged the energies of a sun.

Hitherto quiescent monitors awoke on the bridge. Blank-eyed circlets winked on, needles sprinted ahead, bands ascended on gauges, and a tiny shock ran through every member of the bridge crew.

"All systems," April ordered firmly, "final checkout. Report."

Response came from around the bridge, from speakers at the freshly painted communications station, and finally from Navigation.

"Visual contact, sir. Object approaching on collision course, bearing dead ahead."

"Acknowledged, Lieutenant Po." April addressed the general intercom. "All hands, stand by."

Other, distant hands were standing by in a small room beneath the lunar surface. Other eyes checked chronometers and predictors as they watched the distant Earth-ball, fighting to find a minute speck outlined against that brilliant blue-white globe. The drama begun on a small stage several weeks before was approaching the final curtain.

"Contact in thirty seconds, Captain," Lieutenant Po reported, with an irrepressible shiver of excitement.

"Thank you, Lieutenant."

In suits and ships and stations, thousands of men and women of several races watched their fully formed offspring and waited expectantly.

"Four . . . three . . . ," the navigator counted off tensely, "two . . . one . . . interdiction. . . ."

Head-on, the tiny projectile struck the completed cruiser, exploded, and burst into a small but rapidly expanding ball of brilliance. Tiny reflective fragments caught the morning sunlight and turned the diffusing globe into a spray of diamonds.

Thousands of watching eyes saw the distant explosion and reacted. From electronic pickups set strategically around the assembly area, billions more on Earth and on other globes also saw it—and all reacted.

On billions of speakers, the aged but enormously respected voice of the Federation president, Samuel Solomon Qasr, sounded from a chamber on the moon: "In the name of the United Federation of Planets, for the United Nations of Earth, the Planetary Confederation of Forty Eridani, the United Planets of Sixty-one Cygni, the Star Empire of Epsilon Indii, the Alpha Centauri Concordium of Planets, and all other peace-loving, space-going peoples—I christen thee *Enterprise!*"

Those on board the just-commissioned ship heard those words, but not the cheering of the construction crews gathered around them, or the comments and smiles and expressions of satisfaction on the world below. Though each crew member might have permitted himself a silent observation, of varying content and intensity, these were not voiced aloud.

There was too much to do now.

The Federation Exploration Territory was enormous beyond comprehension, and it was but a minuscule portion of this tiny section of the galaxy. Battle cruisers were too expensive, their personnel too valuable to be tied up on anything as wasteful as a shakedown cruise.

It seemed there was a certain world on the present fringe of Federation expansion which desperately required the know-how and capabilities of a major-class vessel. April had his orders. The initial cruise of the *Enterprise* would be fully operational.

Ceremony concluded, April leaned back in his chair, already a part of him, and called firmly to his helmsman.

"Ahead warp-factor three, Lieutenant Nobis."

It was four decades, forty long years since he had given that first order, April thought. He was still on the bridge of the *Enterprise,* only this day and this place in time he found himself behind the captain's chair, instead of sitting in it.

Still odd, he mused to himself. Odd to be standing here, staring at the familiar—and always overpowering—panorama of stars depicted on the viewscreen ahead and listening to someone else making the entry into the official log.

"Captain's log," the voice was saying, "Stardate 5536.3. The *Enterprise* is on course to the planet Babel, where an inter-Federation ambassadorial gathering is scheduled. Highlight of the conference is to be a ceremony honoring the *Enterprise*'s distinguished passenger."

Kirk paused and glanced behind him to see April still staring quietly at the main screen. The commodore's mind appeared to be elsewhere, but his eyes sparkled as he stared intently at the perfectly ordinary starfield ahead. There was an enthusiasm there that was often absent in officers a third his age. The superstructure might be aged and wrinkled, but Kirk knew the mind it housed was as keen and fascinated with the universe as ever.

Every so often Uhura, Arex, or Sulu would steal a surreptitious glance at their honored guest when they were sure no one was looking. Kirk smiled. A little hero worship would not affect ship efficiency. Besides, he had to admit he wasn't wholly immune to it himself. He turned his attention back to the log. After all, it wasn't every day one had a living legend for an after-dinner chess partner.

"Commodore Robert April," Kirk continued recording, "was the first captain of the U.S.S. *Enterprise* and, for the past twenty years, the Federation ambassador-at-large. Now seventy-five years old, Commodore April has reached mandatory retirement age." Kirk pressed one switch, activated another.

"Captain's log, supplemental to entry of 5536.3. Said retirement age being a bureaucratic abberation— arbitrarily decided on by a cluster of smug civil servants without regard to individual capability or overall

Starfleet efficiency—and a regulation badly in need of overhaul." He clicked off.

"Nice of you to add that, Jim," April approved in soft, almost small-boy tones. "Do you really think anyone will ever pay any attention to it?"

Kirk shook his head. "They had to pick a number, Commodore. How they arrived at seventy-five for everyone human is something I'll never understand. Instead of basing the figure on individual ability and performance, they simply—"

April cut him off smoothly, soothingly. "Oh well. If they didn't have a number, Jim, then there'd be a blank spot on a form some place. And you know what *that* would mean."

Kirk grumbled sarcastically. "The end of Starfleet, I suppose."

"That is hardly likely, Captain. Nor is it logical," Spock observed from across the bridge.

"I guess not, Mr. Spock, but neither is the mandatory retirement setup."

"I never claimed it was, Captain. On Vulcan such things are determined with rather more regard to reason."

"Perhaps it will all change in Starfleet someday, Mr. Spock," April mused hopefully. "Too late for me, I'm afraid." He turned his gaze forward again and was silent for a minute.

"You know, no matter where I've traveled through this galaxy, Jim, this bridge is more home to me than anywhere else. I can't count the number of times these past twenty years when I've turned to give an order to someone and found myself seated across from some utterly bemused diplomat I was negotiating with. It's a wonder I accomplished anything for the Federation." He chuckled. "Most diplomats don't take orders very well—or even suggestions."

"Probably intentional," Kirk observed. "If every one of you behaved reasonably and intelligently at all times, why then all our problems would be quickly solved, and you'd all be out of a job. No more diplomatic corps." April smiled knowingly.

"But as far as this bridge being home," Kirk continued, "yes, I know the feeling myself, Commodore."

"The *Enterprise* has always been like my own child, in a way," April went on. "I was there in San Francisco when her basic components were being built. I consulted with her chief construction engineer, Franz Joseph IV, on her internal configuration. I was present at the orbital assembly plant when they put her innards together.

"When they tested out each newly installed component, whether warp-drive or swimming pool, I was there. The additions and modifications she's taken since are good ones. A ship-of-the-line has to be kept up to date, but . . ." He shrugged. "I miss some of the old-fashioned touches."

"Nostalgia is notoriously inefficient," Spock commented, but so softly no one could hear. He knew an emotional observation when he heard one.

The elevator doors parted to admit Dr. McCoy. He was accompanied by an attractive little woman who projected an air of supreme self-confidence and contentment. Her attire was current high fashion, all emerald green and black and bearing no relationship to Starfleet uniforms. Gray hair, unabashedly untouched, was done up in long taffylike swirls and twists. Even the single flower she carried seemed designed only to complement her. The colorful blossom had petals that wound in and about themselves in an intricate, delicately engineered manner.

The last person in the room she resembled was her husband. Only one thing, besides age, linked them inseparably—both wore that same aura of composure and confidence like a coat of jewels.

For his part, Dr. McCoy wore his standard on-duty uniform and an air of what could best be described as bemused pleasure.

"Jim," he began admiringly, "I didn't realize until now how many of the instruments I use in Sick Bay were originally designed and first used by Sarah. Did you know that she cribbed the first version of the standard cancer monitor together out of some old medical components and phaser-monitor units?"

The woman smiled demurely. "As the first medical officer aboard a ship equipped with warp-drive, it was always necessary for us to come up with new ideas."

"Your modesty is unnecessary, Ms. April," Kirk observed honestly. "Your achievements as a pioneer Starfleet physician are well known and extensively documented. There are many doctors who cannot do what a medical engineer does, and a corresponding number of medical engineers who are ill-prepared to administer treatment. You're one of the few people in Starfleet medicine who ever managed to master the requirements of both professions."

"And it's nice to know," McCoy added, "that the doctor is as beautiful as she is accomplished. A beauty that's reflected by the flower she carries."

"If your medical ability is as accomplished as your flattery, Dr. McCoy, then I know Captain Kirk has no worries in that area of *Enterprise* operations. I won't be impolite and ask if that's a quote—I'll assume you made it up on the spur of the moment." She smiled a youngish smile. "Please feel free to insert such comments wherever you think they fit into the conversation."

Her smile faded as she looked down at the delicate growth in her hands. "I'm afraid, though, that my flower is dying."

So many references to the flower prompted Kirk to turn to get a better look at it. "Let's see ... botanical text, the Reddin catalog ... volume six, which sector ... ?" Mumbling to himself, he thumbed the text. He located it quickly. "A native of Capella Four, isn't it?"

She nodded. "The mature blossom has a lifespan of only a few hours. If you recognize it, Captain, you'll recall how brief the growing period is on that world.

"This is an extreme example even for Capella Four, I'm told. When it was given to me this morning it was a bud barely out of seed. Within a few hours it will be dead." She paused. "It's one of the most beautiful growths in the galaxy, and one of the shortest-lived.

What a pity." She looked up. "I know people like that, too, Captain."

"Excuse me, sir," Spock said in the ensuing silence. "You asked to be notified when we made visual contact with the Beta Niobe Nova."

"Yes . . . thank you, Mr. Spock." Kirk glanced backward. "Ms. April, you're about to see another of the galaxy's most beautiful—and, in astronomical terms, short-lived—sights. Its remnants, though, will last a lot longer than the petals of your flower. The Beta Niobe Nova. Mr. Spock?"

"A moment, Captain, some precision focusing is required." They waited while the first officer made final adjustments at his console. The forward viewscreen blurred, then cleared, to show a monstrous eruption in space, an explosion of primal energy, of raw power— and only incidentally of blazing color.

Yellow and white gases, mutilated matter, glowed at its heart, while at its edges erratic and undisciplined streamers of brilliant red and orange charged blindly into indifferent emptiness. In this isolated section of space, the depressing darkness of the universe was suffused with wild color and wilder energies.

"Magnificent," Sarah April gushed.

"Magnificent and deadly," Spock echoed, "but we are traveling at a safe distance from the nova, Ms. April."

"Beta Niobe, Niobe . . . I've heard that name in connection with the *Enterprise* before." She looked up at the commodore. "Bob, didn't you read me a report some years ago . . . ?"

"Yes . . . you were present when the star first exploded, weren't you, Jim?" he asked.

"We were, Commodore," Kirk replied. "I wasn't aware that in addition to handling all your duties and activities as ambassador-at-large you managed to keep track of such trivia as our day-to-day operations."

April looked at once flattered and embarrassed. "It's not trivia to me, Jim. A part of me will always be on this ship, and the rest of me is intensely interested in what happens to it. Some of your reports to Starfleet headquarters read as anything but uninteresting trivia. As you know, your ship's log is always available to me—a courtesy Starfleet extends to former starship captains. I know what's happening aboard the *Enterprise* as soon as headquarters does.

"If I recall this particular report correctly, you were trapped in a planet's past, about to be tried as a witch just before this star started to go nova."

Kirk nodded. "One of our narrower escapes. For Dr. McCoy and Mr. Spock as well as for me."

"I'll say it was narrow!" McCoy added fervently. "I was trapped in that world's ice age at the time. The only other time in my life I've ever been that cold was when our computer went berserk a little while back and turned the Recreation Chamber into subarctic snowpack."

"Captain . . . ?" A hesitant query from the region of the helm. Kirk looked over absently.

"What is it, Mr. Sulu? Important?"

"I don't know, sir." He looked puzzled. "I've got something moving toward us, at extreme range right now."

Kirk swiveled. "Mr. Spock?"

"No basis for identification as yet, Captain," the first officer replied, staring into the gooseneck viewer. "Vessel is no longer at extreme range, however."

Now it was Kirk's turn to appear confused. "*That* was a quick change. Are you sure, Spock?"

Both curved eyebrows sank as Spock analyzed several readouts at once. "Captain, the object is traveling at a speed nothing short of incredible. Presently on collision course with the *Enterprise*."

Kirk didn't hesitate. "Sound red alert, Lieutenant Uhura. 'Nothing short of incredible' doesn't tell me much, Spock. Spock?"

Crimson warning lights blinked on, accompanied by the appropriate aural blarings.

"Excuse me, Captain," the first officer finally muttered. "You'll have to ascribe my hesitation to sheer incredulity. This object is traveling at a rate theoretically impossible for matter to achieve.

"More specifically—bear in mind I have to override the standard settings, Captain—it is moving at a speed on the order of warp-thirty-six."

The numbers cut through Kirk like a scalpel. "You're right," he finally confessed, "it *is* impossible. Mr. Spock, nothing can travel that fast."

"I fear, Captain, that in this case you must redefine that observation. It is nothing, less one."

"No natural object," April put in, "has ever been recorded as traveling at that speed—or at anything close to it."

"Preliminary sensor reports, Captain," Spock continued, "lead me to an even more astonishing conclusion." He looked up from his instruments. "The object is an artificial construct. I *must* assume it is some kind of ship."

Kirk pondered the information. When he spoke again, his voice was unconsciously hushed. "Who has the technology to build a vessel that can move at that velocity?"

"Obviously, no known race, Captain," Spock pointed out. "Impossible or not, it will make contact with us in one point four minutes."

There was nothing theoretical about the order Kirk gave then. "Hard over, helmsman, change course to a new heading, two full degrees to starboard."

Even as he gave the order he knew that if this ridiculously rapid visitor turned out to be inimical, there was no way they could dodge or outrun it.

The same thought evidently was running through his first officer's mind, because a second later Spock commented, "It is apparently nonbelligerent, Captain. It appears a collision was not intended, as the vessel has not altered its course to match ours.

"If it continues in its present direction, it will plunge directly into the center of the Beta Niobe Nova."

Was that it, then, Kirk thought quickly—a hurried rush to extinction, to suicide? Or was an unknown crew injured, its ship damaged?

"Lieutenant Uhura," he called over his shoulder,

"open hailing frequencies. I want to talk to that ship's captain—if it has one."

A long pause while Uhura worked at her console. Finally she turned, spoke discouragingly. "I'm sorry, Captain. I've sent everything in its direction except carrier pigeons. If there's anyone on board capable of responding, they've elected not to."

Kirk pondered. "Have you tried all the emergency frequencies, Lieutenant?"

"Sir, I've broadcast on every possible frequency for every listed race, and a few that are only hypothetical. No response."

"Vessel is nearing a parallel course, Captain," Sulu reported uneasily—uneasily because their brief course change was now taking them toward the raging nova instead of past it.

"Increase speed to warp-seven, Mr. Sulu, try to stay with it as much as possible."

"Aye, sir."

"Despite our best efforts, the alien vessel will shoot past us very shortly, Captain," Spock declared.

"I realize that, Spock." His voice dropped to a murmur. "It may be that they can't communicate—maybe their communications equipment's been damaged. Perhaps the entire crew is injured. We've got to find out, somehow."

"It'll have to be soon, sir," Sulu noted. "She'll go right out of range as soon as she parallels us."

"Then we'll have to slow her down. Mr. Sulu, put our forward tractor beam on that ship as soon as it comes within range. Full power."

"Is that advisable, Captain?" Spock wondered aloud.

"It's more advisable than letting a possibly friendly crew burn to a crisp in the nova, Mr. Spock. If I were injured and aboard that vessel, I'd want any stranger to lend a hand. If they know what they're doing and insist on committing suicide . . . well, let's evaluate that possibility last of all."

"It is not that, Captain," Spock protested. "I agree with you completely on the possibility that the crew may be incapacitated or that their broadcast instrumentation is damaged beyond use. If that is the case, then naturally we must do everything in our power to aid them. My worry is that we may overextend ourselves in doing so. I am particularly concerned about the aftereffects of locking a tractor beam on an object moving at such a velocity. To understate the matter, there could be severe physical repercussions. Such a thing has never been tried before."

"Naturally not, Mr. Spock, the opportunity never arose before. It'll be history in a few seconds, whatever the result. Mr. Sulu?"

"Forward tractor beam energized, Captain." A pause; then, "Contact achieved . . . locked on."

"Any effect?"

"Sir," Sulu responded after a quick check of his readouts, "I'm running it at maximum power, but the alien is still moving on the same course."

"Tractor beam monitors report no damage to components or tractor bracing," Spock reported evenly. "No sign of dangerous stress apparent yet."

It was Arex's turn to speak up. The quiet navigator made his first comment on the proceedings. "We are apparently having some effect on the vessel's mobility, Captain, if not its course. Using the parameters employed by Mr. Spock, it would appear that the other ship's speed has dropped to the equivalent of warp-twenty-seven."

"Darn well froze it in its tracks," Kirk muttered. "That's *some* ship."

That was when Uhura's excited voice commanded all the attention on the bridge.

"Captain, we're being beamed!"

II

"I can't be certain—the message is terribly scrambled, and like nothing I've ever seen before—but I *think* it's a request to open intership communications," Uhura declared.

"So much for the disability and damage theory," Kirk observed tautly. "That means they're probably healthy—just antisocial. Switch on the screen, Uhura."

The communications officer appeared to be struggling with her instrumentation, but eventually the view of the grand nova vanished. It was replaced by a portrait of a more composed subject, but one in its own way no less fascinating.

As usual, Kirk awaited this first view of an unknown race without preconceived imagery. Even so, the first sight of a representative of supreme warp-drive technology was at once disappointing and shocking. Disappointing because its manipulator was no wizened alien genius, and shocking because the reality tended to the other extreme. In fact, the young woman who appeared on the screen was so human that she could have traded uniforms with Uhura or any of the *Enterprise*'s female complement and moved freely about the ship.

When she spoke, however, her speech was anything but familiar. Nothing sounded normal; even the inflections seemed intentionally misplaced.

"Demood eb yam I ro ecno ta pihs ym esaeler, ssergorp ym gniwols si maeb ruoy, noissim ytiroirp a no mI."

Following this urgent stream of decidedly incomprehensible alien chatter, the viewscreen once again went dark. It was replaced automatically by the view forward—the steadily growing magnificence of the Beta Niobe Nova.

20

"Human, certainly," Kirk ventured, "unless her race is a shape-changer."

"It would have to be more than that, Captain," Spock observed, "to mimic so precisely without ever having contacted us."

"Possibly even a direct human analog," the captain continued, "though the likeness appears too exact to be true. The only thing that doesn't match up is her language. Never heard anything like that before. Yet somehow it sounds vaguely familiar. I could swear she referred to herself as 'I' at least once."

"It might merely have been the 'aye' sound, Jim," April suggested from behind him. "I didn't recognize the language, either. I haven't heard speech like that, not in all my travels throughout the galaxy. But as you say, it did have something familiar about it. Strange."

"Let's see if the ship's translator can come up with identification, Lieutenant Uhura," ordered Kirk.

"All right, sir."

As she ran the tape of the woman's brief speech through that intricate portion of the *Enterprise*'s computer system, she also allowed the sounds to play over the bridge speakers. Once again everyone listened to that oddly pitched, weirdly modulated, yet faintly familiar babble. Repetition failed to produce enlightenment; no one could make any more sense out of the situation this time than before.

A pause after it trailed off, then, "Negative response, Captain," she finally reported. "Whatever it is, it's no known language in our section of the galaxy."

"Implement decoding procedures," came the command. "Might be a coded variant of some little-known humanoid speech."

The woman on the screen hadn't delivered her message as if it were in code, Kirk thought as Uhura worked. She had delivered her sentence—if that's what it was—rapidly and without apparent effort, as though it were her natural, everyday speech. Furthermore, she had done so in a fashion suggesting that her listeners would understand instantly.

There was surprise and just a hint of embarrassment

in Uhura's voice when she spoke again. "I've got the answer, Captain. I should have recognized the pattern right away, but it was a little too close to home. The woman was speaking our own language, only in reverse."

"Reverse," Arex echoed from the navigation station. "No wonder it sounded so familiar, like a tape played backward."

"Correct," Kirk agreed sourly—he should have identified it himself—"only without the distortions one would expect of such a playback.

"All right, Uhura, let's hear that tape again, only backward this time—that should sound forward to us. And put the visual tape on screen again, too."

Uhura nodded. Once more they saw the anxious face of the woman, once more listened to her tense message. Only this time it was easily understandable, even though her words failed to match her mouth movements.

"I'm on a priority mission," the words tumbled out, "your beam is slowing my progress. Release my ship at once or I may be doomed."

"Short and to the point. Open hailing frequency again, Lieutenant, matching ours to her broadcast. Tell her she's endangering her life if she continues on her present course, and explain why. Tape it and then broadcast it in reverse, so she'll understand. Though it's beyond me," he continued puzzledly, "how anyone could head for the heart of a nova and not have an inkling there just might be a bit of danger involved. Something doesn't make sense here." A sudden thought intervened.

"Mr. Spock, we should be close enough to obtain a decent internal sensor scan. How many life forms aboard that vessel?"

"I have just concluded a check of our first readings, Captain. The result is conclusive: There is only one. The woman we saw on the screen."

"No response, sir," Uhura broke in. "She's incapable of replying—or else is just refusing to."

Kirk was about to suggest another approach when a

demanding buzz from his armchair intercom caught his attention.

"Engineering to bridge. Engineering to bridge."

"Yes, Scotty, what is it?"

"Captain, I'm gettin' severe stress reports from all over the ship. The *Enterprise* wasn't meant to travel at such a speed."

What speed, Kirk wondered.

Scott rushed on. "If we keep on like this, we'll break up, Captain."

"Just a minute, Scotty." Kirk looked ahead. "Sulu, are we still holding on with that tractor?"

The helmsman checked his readouts. "Holding firm, Captain."

That explained it, then. "Lieutenant Arex, we are apparently being towed. What is our present speed?"

"Warp-eleven, sir," the Edoan replied incredulously, after a frantic check of his instrumentation.

"No wonder Scotty's having trouble. Mr. Spock, how long before the alien vessel impinges on the outermost danger zone, the first lethal radiation?"

Spock made a quick check and performed some rapid calculations. "Three minutes, forty-two seconds plus, Captain. There may be some local variance in field strength, but generally speaking . . ."

Kirk spoke hurriedly to the chair pickup again. "Scotty?"

"I heard, Captain."

"We'd burn up in the nova before our superstructure went. I'm trying to stop that ship from destroying itself."

"Well and noble, Captain," the chief engineer agreed, "but speakin' of destroyin' oneself, keep in mind we can't travel like this much longer."

"Three and half minutes, Scotty, that's all. Give me that. Kirk out."

And he cut off, leaving the chief to oversee some frenzied emergency bracing of the warp-drive engines.

"Speed still increasing, Captain," Arex reported. "Warp-fourteen, warp-fifteen . . ."

Seconds before, they were traveling at warp-eleven,

and even that was putting a severe strain on the ship. It also meant that the engines on board that tiny suicidal craft were even more powerful than first imagined—they were slowly overcoming the drag effect of the *Enterprise*'s tractor.

Kirk had no choice but to release that beam. There was a point beyond which he wasn't willing to go to rescue the confused or misguided pilot of the other ship, and that point had been reached. The *Enterprise* must not be risked.

"Cancel the tractor, Mr. Sulu. Lieutenant Uhura, continue beaming our message at the other ship until they acknowledge or . . ."—he hesitated—". . . until they become incapable of acknowledging. That gives you about three minutes. When she hits those first radiation belts, her instrumentation's going to fry. Maybe she'll at least change course a little."

"Yes, sir," Uhura said doubtfully. "I'll beam it, sir, but . . ."

"Captain . . . ?" There was a strained note in Sulu's voice. It brought Kirk's head around quickly. "I can't release the tractor."

"Explain, Mr. Sulu. Fast."

Sulu stared helplessly at his console. "All controls appear inoperative—the ship isn't responding as she should."

"Take it easy, Lieutenant. Go to manual override."

The helmsman's hands flashed over the console, repeated the necessary manipulations again, then a third time. "Still no response, sir. We're locked tight." A touch of panic was creeping into his voice now.

"We've got to break that beam," Kirk said tightly.

"Our speed is now warp-twenty," Spock announced quietly. "Alien vessel will contact first lethal radiation in one minute, fifty seconds."

"Never mind that now," Kirk shouted. "Mr. Spock, see if you can aid Mr. Sulu." The first officer moved rapidly to the helm. "Lieutenant Uhura, contact Security and have them break out a phaser rifle. I want the tractor-beam components melted into a tin puddle!"

Even as he gave the order he knew there was no way Security could break out the necessary equipment, set up, and perform the required destruction before they passed the point of no return. They needed those three and half minutes again, and now they didn't have even half that.

He swiveled in the chair, resigned. "I'm sorry, Commodore, Dr. April. It looks as if we're not going to make this conference."

He saw that further words were unnecessary. The commodore and his wife were probably the most relaxed people on the bridge. It was a serenity derived from having faced death a dozen times before. Anyone who served on a far-ranging starship knew that life was at best a transitory business.

"Captain," April told him, "as Starfleet personnel we were always prepared to give up what small sentience life has granted us. I was ready for the end before I ever set foot on my first ship."

"We're still starship personnel, Captain," Sarah April added softly, holding tight to the now wilting flower.

"We do have one chance left," a grim-faced Kirk explained. "After it enters the first zone of strong radiation, the alien ship should burn up rapidly. With nothing to lock onto, our tractor beam will be freed." He turned toward the science station.

"Mr. Spock, will we have enough time to apply full braking power and execute the necessary course change?"

Spock considered the question in light of the constantly changing information the ship's sensors supplied. "We're up to warp-twenty-four and still increasing speed rapidly, Captain. But I calculate that we will have forty-two point eight five seconds to effect a significant course change following destruction of the alien vessel. That is assuming, of course, that it does not possess radiation screens as advanced as its engines."

Kirk had no time to reflect on that possibility. "Mr.

Sulu, I want a course implemented at warp-eight the moment our tractor is released."

"Yes, sir. Bearing, sir?"

"Whatever will get us clear of here the quickest—this is no time to be choosy."

Sulu nodded, then punched the necessary information into the *Enterprise*'s helm. Kirk hit the intercom again.

"Mr. Scott, we're going to try to slow our speed a little. Stand by to apply full braking power in fifty seconds."

"Standing by, Captain," Scott acknowledged. "A good thing, too."

"Fifty-two seconds to contact for the other ship, Captain," Spock declared.

Kirk studied the view on the screen ahead. Detectors still showed the tail end of the tiny alien craft. It seemed incapable of mounting engines equipped to drive it at such incredible velocities. It was almost lost against the now frighteningly near blaze of red, orange-yellow, and white fluorescing gases.

"Eighteen ... twelve, eleven," the first officer was counting off.

"Stand by to execute course change, Mr. Sulu. No time to spare. Apply maximum braking power."

"Braking," Sulu announced. The fading silhouette of the alien ship had vanished now, subsumed by a licking tongue of orange phosphorescence.

"Now, Sulu," Kirk snapped, unable to restrain giving the verbal command even though he knew the *Enterprise*'s electronic nerves were prekeyed to perform the necessary maneuver.

"Something's wrong, Captain!" Sulu yelled immediately. "We're still being pulled by the alien ship!"

"Impossible, impossible," Kirk murmured. "There shouldn't be anything left for the tractor beam to lock onto. By now that tiny craft and its enigmatic pilot should have been reduced to cinders."

"We're still connected by tractor to something, Captain," announced Arex, "and we're still building speed."

"Contact with destructive energy levels in thirty-five seconds," declared a dispassionate Spock, eyes never straying from his instruments.

"Incredible engineering," Kirk mumbled. "A ship that small capable of warp-thirty-six. If her people can build engines like that, maybe they *have* invented shielding sufficient to permit a ship to survive the heat and radiation of a nova. But the *Enterprise* can't."

He knew the answer, but decided there was nothing to be lost by a last check. "Mr. Scott, we are receiving full braking power, aren't we?"

"Aye, sir," the answer came back, "but we're as bad off as before. As long as we're locked to that little skiff, or whatever it is, I canna do nothin' with the engines."

"Contact in twenty seconds," Spock informed him solemnly.

"Mr. Sulu . . . ?"

"Still no change, sir. We're still locked in. Warp-speed . . . warp-thirty-five."

Kirk was out of the command chair and at the helmsman's side in a second, keying controls himself. It was a last, desperate hope. Even the most experienced officer could overlook . . . overlook what? What could he hope to find that both Sulu and Spock had missed?

Some minuscule calculation, some fail-safe forgotten, ignored.

"It's *got* to work," he muttered to himself as he furiously manipulated useless controls.

"Fourteen seconds," counted Spock inexorably. "Thirteen, twelve . . ."

Kirk returned to his seat, turning slowly as he sat. At least they would not die in darkness. The awesome, overpowering glory of the nova's heart was sucking them in at incredible speed.

"No use. It's finished."

Behind him, Robert April had unobtrusively slipped an arm around his wife's shoulders. Her hands clutched a little tighter around the nearly dead blossom.

"Three . . . two . . . one . . . ," Spock concluded.

Something picked the *Enterprise* up and heaved it forward, bounced it off a rubbery surface, and threw it once more. Those on the bridge bobbed about like rubber toys in a bathtub. A dizzying assortment of color swirled about the ship, but no one had the time or inclination to notice—everyone was too busy trying to keep from being tossed against a bulkhead or neighbor as the ship rode out a tremendous buffeting.

Kirk reflected on the fact that there shouldn't have been any buffeting, let alone anyone still alive to feel it. By now the *Enterprise* should have been nothing but a rapidly diffusing field of ruptured molecules melting into the raging energies of Beta Niobe.

The ship slowly ceased its violent shaking. And yet, Kirk mused as he rose slowly to his feet from where he had been thrown, they were still here, still alive, and, from the looks of the bridge, still functioning. He saw his shocked surprise mirrored in the faces of the other officers as they found themselves intact. Slowly, stations were resumed by dazed personnel.

"What happened?" Uhura finally wondered aloud.

"A great many things, Lieutenant," Spock declared. He was working at his station with an intenseness unusual even for him.

Uhura was unable to request a more specific explanation, because Kirk had called for damage reports. They came in immediately and constituted another surprise. All decks reported no damage, no injuries other than a few minor bumps and scrapes to personnel from being violently thrown about.

Kirk's amazement grew. Everyone still alive, and healthy as well.

Of course, he still had no idea what had happened to them, or where they were cruising at the moment. At any instant the ship might come apart at the seams, as should have happened several minutes before. He shrugged mentally. No point in dwelling on that. Maybe they would at least be spared enough time to figure out what had happened to them.

"Lieutenant Uhura, can you get us any external visuals?"

"I'll try, sir." Some very peculiar static rippled

across the main viewscreen, then cleared without warning.

Or had it?

Kirk blinked, but the image that had appeared on the screen was still there, unwavering, unchanged, unbelievable. It was as impressive as it was impossible, in its own bizarre way. What Kirk and Spock and everyone else saw was a normal-looking universe, normal except for one slight change.

It was a universe of pure white, speckled with stars of varying intensities of black.

"Where are we?" April whispered in amazement.

"I don't . . ." Kirk paused, noticing a new aberration. The starfield on the screen was shrinking away, not moving past. A quick check of instrumentation confirmed his observation. The *Enterprise* was traveling back-end first through this perverse vacuum.

"I believe, Captain," Spock hypothesized aloud as he stared at the negative panorama ahead, "that we have somehow passed into an alternate universe, normal in every respect—but normal in reverse of what we know to be real. We have entered a universe where everything is the opposite of our own."

"Black stars in a white void," Kirk murmured. "It looks frightening, somehow."

"Physics are never frightening, Captain. Merely hard work sometimes."

"Mr. Sulu," Kirk asked firmly, "what's our present situation?"

"Still apparently locked onto the alien ship, Captain."

Kirk turned to his first officer. "Radiation?"

"Nothing, Captain," Spock announced after a moment's check of his gauges. "It seems we're no longer in any danger. I wonder if we ever were."

Kirk thought of one more detail to be checked. "Bridge to Engineering . . . Scotty, how are we holding up?"

"It was hectic for a few minutes, sir. What's going on? Everything's workin' properly—but in reverse. We're havin' to learn how to run the ship all over again, backward. Takes a minute to get used to it. Not the instrumentation adjustments; it's the goin' against years of experience, pushin' *off* when you want *on*, turnin' to maximum when you want to shut somethin' down. I know when I adjust the engine flux backward now that everythin's goin' to be all right, but I canna keep from feelin' in my bones that I'm goin' to blow us to kingdom come."

"Take your time and do the best you can, Scotty," Kirk sympathized. "Speaking of the engines . . . ?"

"They shouldn't still be with us, Captain, but they are. Don't ask me how or why. They should have torn free of their pylons a long time ago, considerin' the strain on them."

"Thank you, Scotty. Keep a close watch and let me know if our status changes."

"Aye, sir. Engineering out."

"Now then, Lieutenant Uhura, we're going to contact our closed-mouthed alien-human friend again." The firmness in his tone indicated that this time silence wouldn't be accepted. "We need some answers, and a universe-sized explanation. That pilot is the only one around who can provide them for us."

"Captain Kirk!"

He spun, to see a wide-eyed Dr. April gesturing with something in her hands.

"I'm sure Captain Kirk has other problems to consider at the moment besides the state of your gift, dear," the commodore observed.

"Then he'd better consider this new one, Bob. Look at it. You too, Captain—everyone."

Somehow in the midst of the dire emergency it seemed only proper to find herself staring at a flower. But Dr. April's concern was well-founded.

"Before we entered this negative universe, extra dimension or whatever this is, this bloom was on the verge of dying. Now look at it—it's in full bloom again!"

Indeed, a glance was sufficient to show the brilliant blossom bursting forth with apparently new, waxy petals and glistening young stamen. It had regained the color it had when the Aprils had boarded the *Enterprise* . . . and more.

"It doesn't make sense," Kirk finally commented, "which only makes sense here, I suppose. If everything else is backward . . ."

"It's more than a regeneration, Captain," she went on. "It's almost as if it were growing younger again. I can feel the regeneration as I'm holding it."

"Feel it . . . you can see it," Sulu declared.

Even as they watched the blossom began to shrink again, the petals pulling in on themselves, as the flower commenced its return toward the small, hard bud from which it had originally sprung.

"Captain," Spock put in, "I suspect that Dr. April's flower is not the only thing on board that is growing younger."

"What do you mean, Mr. Spock?"

"To start, Captain, you might note that the ship's chronometers are running backward."

Kirk stared down at his own wrist instrument. He watched the second hand methodically tick off time in a counterclockwise direction. As he watched, he could see the minute hand slowly edging backward as well.

The full alienness of the situation in which they found themselves was driven home more powerfully by this simple alteration of an everyday event—the measuring of time—than by the view of black stars spotted across white space.

"Time as well as physics is apparently reversed here, Captain," the first officer concluded.

"One crisis at a time, Spock."

Uhura called to him. "The alien ship is finally responding to our call, Captain. I have visual contact established, ready to put on the screen."

"Please do so, Lieutenant."

Once more the portrait of the alien pilot appeared before them. Only this time, when she spoke, the words sounding on the speakers matched her mouth movements, and Kirk found he could understand her perfectly.

"Your actions almost cost me my life, and your own

as well." She was obviously still confused as to why the *Enterprise* had interfered. "Why didn't you release my ship as I asked?"

"This poses an interesting physical and semantic question, Captain," mused Spock. "Are we understanding her speech because she is speaking backward but our thought processes are reversed?"

"We can debate it later, Mr. Spock. At the moment, the only thing I'm interested in reversing for sure is our presence here."

But the alien pilot *had* posed a question.

"I'm Captain James T. Kirk, commanding the U.S.S. *Enterprise*. We tried to prevent you from entering the Beta Niobe Nova because it has been our experience in the past that vessels which enter novas are never heard from again. We thought that you might have been injured, or your ship's navigation helm crippled. We had no reason to believe," he continued drily, "that your vessel was equipped to withstand such forces. For that matter, we didn't expect our own ship could, either. We attempted to disengage our tractor beam at the last minute, but were unable to do so."

"I see. Your gesture was gallant and well-meaning, but wholly unnecessary. I had to return to my own universe, Captain Kirk. In order to do so, it was necessary for my ship to pass through the distortion fields and stress energies of what you call the Beta Niobe Nova, in order to emerge into my universe from the new star, Amphion."

"New star? Mr. Spock, check our readings aft."

Spock looked up a moment later and nodded in confirmation of the pilot's claim. "It seems to be so, Captain. Instead of a nova, retracing our course leads us back into what appears to be a very new, very black star."

"Who are you," Kirk asked the flat, solemn face on the screen, "and how did you come to be in our universe in the first place?"

"I am a solitary explorer—Karla Five, I am called. I was caught unawares when Amphion, previously a dead star, abruptly went nova and came to life. I was pulled in by the explosively expanding gravitational field. Instead of burning up, I passed into a universe where everything operates in reverse of my own."

"Our universe," Kirk said.

"I wandered helplessly for several months, but never losing track of the place where I had emerged into your universe," she continued. "Endless calculations led me to a single conclusion: The only chance I had of returning home was to pass back at maximum acceleration through the exploding star, your nova. And then at that last moment, you happened on a ship you thought was in distress, and were drawn in with me. I am sorry."

"You mentioned your calculations," Spock reminded her. "What is your explanation for this transuniverse effect?"

"Tentative, certainly," Karla Five explained. "It would appear that the forces at the heart of a nova generate sufficient spatial stress to create a bridge between our two universes. A vessel moving toward this shifting bridge at a sufficient speed will pass from universe to universe rapidly enough to avoid the dangerous energies which exist in such centers."

Behind Kirk, Commodore April listened to Karla Five's theory with astonishment and admiration. "In her universe, then, a nova is a dead star which comes to life, whereas in ours it's one which is going through its death throes in a violent manner. When these two differently defined events take place at a particular point in space, it is possible to travel between the two. This discovery could revolutionize cosmology."

"*If* we can get back to tell it to anyone," Kirk reminded him. "And the way to do that seems pretty obvious. We have to go back the way we came, through the double nova."

Karla Five looked troubled. "Would that I could be sure such a thing was possible, Captain Kirk. Amphion was not a full-sized burning sun when I was drawn into it. That has changed. I would not think it possible to dive into the heart of a live sun and survive."

"We'd think the same thing of a full-sized nova, which is what Beta Niobe is," Kirk countered.

"True, Captain. Even so, the question of our return is apparently not a simple matter of retracing our steps. We must examine the alternatives more intensely."

"What would you suggest, Mr. Spock?"

"Some additional time to consider the physics of the matter, and if possible to study the information produced by Karla Five's computer."

"Naturally I'll give all the aid I can, as will my people," the alien pilot told them. "I am now proceeding to my home world of Arret, Captain Kirk. I suggest you set a course to follow my ship."

"That shouldn't be difficult," Kirk replied, "seeing as how we're still attached to you by our tractor beam." She looked grim, shook her head.

Of course, that undoubtedly constituted a friendly gesture here, Kirk reminded himself. Unless she was concerned about something else. Unless his own optic nerves were also working in reverse, feeding him backward information. Or . . .

He shook his head. There were ramifications to their present situation that could drive a man mad.

"Mr. Sulu, plot a following course. And keep trying to disengage that tractor beam. Meanwhile call off the security detail—no point in destroying the tractor mechanism now."

"Aye aye, sir."

"Mr. Spock, get with your people in Life Sciences and see if they can verify that everyone on board is growing younger. Also the rate at which such reverse aging is taking place—if in fact that's what's happening to us."

It didn't take long for the efficient instruments and technicians of the great cruiser to verify that that was precisely what was happening.

Kirk considered the news calmly, finally glancing up from his command position. "Well, there you have it, everyone. I'm sure none of us minds growing younger instead of older for a change."

Silence.

"It pleases me anyway, Jim," April finally said. "If we could remain in this universe long enough, I'd no longer be at the mandatory retirement age."

"Let's not lose sight of our present position, Commodore. We must return home. I'm open to suggestions. Spock?"

"There seems only one reasonably sure way, Captain," he explained quietly. "We must reproduce, as exactly as possible, the conditions which carried Karla Five's ship from her universe into ours. Two novas must occupy the same space in both universes in order to create the proper gateway. The difficulty here has already been pinpointed by Karla Five.

"We must locate a star in the process of being born, which must also coincide with a nova in our own galaxy. As she has pointed out, Amphion is now a raging furnace, a growing star. We cannot chance returning via the same route."

April was shaking his head. "The chances of our doing that even if we had time to scan this whole negative galaxy . . . no, Mr. Spock, the odds are too high to compute."

"I must disagree with your evaluation of our chances, Commodore. I have already computed the odds. They are on the order of fifty-two million to one."

Kirk grinned tightly . . . or did he frown, and have it reversed here? No way of knowing. "At least we have a chance."

Heated discussion followed, which included most of the engineering officers and astrophysics technicians. Various suggestions were made; one was to detach the *Enterprise*'s saucer and main living quarters and use the warp-drive engines to overload, thus generating a new star in this universe.

Scott vetoed the idea, pointing out vociferously that they were not in the business of making stars, that the physics were doubtful, that there was no way they could be certain of aligning their artificially generated sun with an existing nova in the positive universe—and besides, without the warp-drive engines they might not get up enough speed to make the dangerous passage in time to prevent total destruction.

The suggestion, along with the others, was tabled. Most were more fantastic than reasonable, requiring gigantic amounts of energy beyond the *Enterprise*'s ability to produce.

Nevertheless, discussions continued throughout the ship, even as they entered orbit around Karla Five's home world of Arret.

"Message coming in, Captain," Uhura announced. "Karla Five is asking if you're prepared to beam down to her world."

"Indicate that we'll be down shortly. Commodore April, Mr. Spock, and I will comprise the landing party."

Kirk rose from his chair and headed for the turbolift, April following. They arrived in the Transporter Room to find Scott waiting for them, prepared to handle the transporter chores himself. But the chief engineer could not disguise a worried frown.

"Something the matter, Scotty? Karla Five *has* given us coordinates to beam down?"

"Aye, sir, she has that."

The three officers moved to the transporter alcove. "Well," Kirk prompted, "why the hesitation, Scotty? I know when something's on your mind."

"It's just, Captain, that . . . well, she identifies the location as her son's laboratory."

Kirk's forehead furrowed. He considered the obvious youth of Karla Five, his ship's desperate situation, and understood the cause of Scott's concern.

"I see what you mean, Scotty. We don't have time for kid games right now. But these people live in a peculiar universe. Their sense of humor might be somewhat backward, too. Anyhow, those are the coordinates she gave. I suspect we're going to need her help to get out of this. Let's not give unnecessary offense. Beam us down, Mr. Scott."

"Aye, sir," Scott acknowledged, looking unhappy. He moved the appropriate levers and dials.

A high whine sounded in the chamber, shrill and familiar. But the corresponding sensation of molecular dissolution was absent. Kirk glanced down, saw himself still standing, solid as ever, on the transporter disk. He looked questioningly at the transporter console, but Scott seemed equally puzzled.

"I dinna understand it, Captain. I'm running through the usual sequence. Everything checks out operational, but—"

Spock interrupted. "The key word is 'usual,' Mr. Scott. Reverse the procedure. Beam us *up* from the provided coordinates."

"But you're already . . . ach, of course! I should know by now."

Reversing the standard transporter sequence produced three properly glittering pillars of light within the alcove.

III

Kirk, Spock, and Commodore April materialized on the steps of a two-story modern structure. A short glance around indicated that they were located on the outskirts of a fair-sized metropolis.

The buildings around them, and in the distant urban area, were decidedly different. Not unattractively so, Kirk noted approvingly. They were clearly designed for normal-sized, normally proportioned humanoids. Only the aesthetic approach was different.

Leaning back, Kirk squinted at the sky. It was blue, but with an alien suggestion of bright green. Somewhere above it, he knew, it faded into a white canopy against which an orphaned *Enterprise* orbited forlornly.

"Good evening, gentlemen."

Karla Five was standing in the entrance to the building, squinting at them and smiling. "I'm sorry you had to arrive on Arret in the middle of the night."

Kirk began to wonder if his mind was running in circles now as well as in reverse. "Middle of the night?" he echoed. "The sun is shining in our faces."

"I beg your pardon, Captain?" Karla Five looked amused. "What a funny thing to say. The moon is quite visible. See?" And she indicated the dark purple orb which dominated the sky.

Kirk stared. "You'll have to excuse me, I'm still not used to reversing everything. It takes some getting used to."

"No need to explain, Captain Kirk," she replied. "I know exactly what you're going through. At least you have the company of others to help you. When I was thrown unexpectedly into your universe I nearly went mad. Imagine seeing brightly colored stars against *black* space. Horrible, unnatural sight!

"Anyway," she assured them, "the sun will come up

soon and it will be dark again. Please come into my son's laboratory. I've awakened him, and he's already hard at work on your problem."

The interior of the house was as pleasant as the exterior, filled with many full-grown plants undoubtedly growing younger. Karla Five led them to a large, spacious chamber. The walls were lined with star-maps—all black on white, of course.

They proceeded to a small, rectangular construct set in the far corner of the vast, domed room. Closer inspection revealed its identity. There was nothing mysterious about it, and since it was exactly what it appeared to be, Kirk thought it utterly out of place in the extensively equipped lab.

It was a playpen, and it was occupied now by a small child. The infant was surrounded by toys, a plastic bottle of liquid, and numerous other less readily identifiable items.

At the moment the child was on its unsteady, stubby legs, playing with a rattling attachment secured to the side of the crib.

Kirk noticed a man in his fifties working nearby. He nodded on noticing Kirk's gaze, then adjusted his lab coat and went back to realigning the chart slides he was projecting on a far section of wall.

"With all respect," April commented, also noticing the busy adult, "how can a woman as young as you have a son old enough to be accomplished in the sciences?"

Karla Five's surprise seemed genuine. "I'm astonished that a young man like yourself would ask such a question, Commodore April. Allow me to introduce my son, Karl Four."

Kirk was beginning to wonder if he was expected to shake hands with the infant, when the older man approached them.

"I'm honored to meet you, gentlemen," he began. "I've read my mother's tapes of her encounter with you in the other universe, and how you come to be here. I hope I can help."

Spock was explaining even as Kirk tried once more to readjust his thinking.

"Eminently logical, you see. Since the flow of time is reversed here, then it is natural for one to be born at an advanced age and to die in infancy. Your descendants," he said to Karl Four, "are born before you, and your ancestors after. I should like to see some local obstetrical—"

"Please, Mr. Spock," Kirk interrupted, a mite desperately, "let's stick to physics."

"If this is your son," April inquired, "then who is the chap in the playpen?"

"Karl Six, of course," she explained easily. "My father. He's led a long and healthy life, made many contributions to our people in the sciences." She shook her head—happily? Sadly, Kirk corrected himself.

"I'm afraid most of his knowledge is gone now. He has entered senile infancy."

"You mean he no longer has it?" wondered Kirk.

Karla Five made a gesture. "I mean our society no longer has it. As our race evolves, all knowledge is lost . . . the natural order of things."

"More and more fascinating," declared a thoroughly enchanted Spock. "A race begins with all the knowledge it will ever have, and as it evolves, the knowledge is progressively lost. Progressive regression."

"We could remain eternally awed at the differences between our universes and civilizations," Kirk snapped briskly, "but we have to find a method of returning to our own universe."

"Exactly what I've been devoting all my time to since Karla Five beamed me the details of your difficulty," Karl Four told them. He gestured. "If you'll direct your attention to the far wall. . . ."

As they turned, he moved to a small panel and adjusted the switches on it. The wall across the chamber seemed to vanish. In its place was a three-dimensional cube looking for all the world like a gigantic block of glassy chocolate-chip ice cream.

"This is an in-depth map of our galaxy—at least, the

portion of it we have explored," Karl Four explained.
"Our home system, and Arret, is here."

As he spoke, one of the black flecks near the cube's
center brightened—or was it darkened?

"And you entered our universe through the new
star, the Amphion Nova . . . here." A minuscule distance away from the first, a second black fleck pulsed
noticeably.

Kirk studied the exquisite detail of the map carefully. "Somehow we have to coordinate this with our
own charts, match the location of known novas in our
universe to potential birthing stars here. Mr. Spock?"

"I foresee no difficulty, Captain. All physical laws
appear to operate uniformly here, only in opposition to
those we know. Therefore, distances and speeds in this
universe should conform to our own. Karl Four, if I
could have a look at the workings of your chart projector, and an explanation . . ."

"At your service, sir," the Arretian scientist responded.

Several hours of study and numerous exchanges of information with the Engineering Department brought
results in the form of several specially modified chart-
spools beamed down from the orbiting starship.

They should have functioned, according to Spock's
design, in the Arretian navigational computer, but they
did not. They failed even to activate it.

It was April who suggested the solution. "How soon
we forget. Try running your computer in reverse, Karl
Four. It should accept our information then."

And so it was. Everything went smoothly after that.

"Incredible, the degree of parallel," Karl Four murmured continually. "I wonder which universe will meet
its end first. Yours, which is aging, or ours, which becomes progressively more youthful. I wonder if the
nova–nova bridge is the only physical interrelation between our universes. I wonder," he mused, "what the
theological relationships might be?"

"Maybe someday we'll have time to find out," ventured Kirk. "Right now, it's the nova–nova bridge I'm
interested in."

"Assuming Beta Niobe and the Amphion sun here do match up on the two charts, Mr. Spock," wondered April aloud, "*can* we locate similar potential occurrences in both universes?"

Spock replied thoughtfully. "I believe so, Commodore, provided the Arretian navigational equipment will continue to process *Enterprise* information as efficiently as it has thus far."

Karl Four adjusted the chart projector once again. Kirk started in spite of himself when the huge map shifted suddenly to a black cube with colored stars hung within. Nor could he fail to notice the way Karl Four jumped at the appearance of the, to him, perverse sight—one which contradicted all his own laws of nature.

"A direct match-up," said Spock, indicating the second still-pulsing pinpoint. "Beta Niobe ... Amphion on the negative-universe chart. Plotting from there ... have you some kind of probe, sir?"

Karl Four hunted in a cabinet until he produced a long, thin metal rod. He handed it to Spock, who inserted it into the black cube, moving it slowly forward through space and stars with equal facility, until the tip stopped near a small star.

"This should be Vulcan."

The Arretian pressed a switch, and the system Spock had located glowed brightly. Again the pointer moved, slightly.

"And here, Earth."

"Amazing," Karla Five said. She nodded to her son, who switched back to the Arretian chart. "It corresponds exactly to Arret." Back to the color-on-black universe of the Federation. Kirk found himself growing a little dizzy as they switched universes by the minute.

"I would like to visit my Vulcan analog," Spock declared, studying the glowing points within the cube projection. "Perhaps someday it will be possible."

"If we don't get out of here, Mr. Spock, you'll have a chance to do more visiting than you want."

"That anxious I am not, Captain." The first officer turned his attention back to the chart, gesturing with the long pointer for all the world like a schoolmaster lecturing a class of youngsters.

"It is now possible to determine with reasonable accuracy the position of simultaneous novas in the two universes, with more ease than I thought would be the case. If . . . ," and he looked back at Karl Four, "you can coordinate both maps at the same time."

The Arretian thought hard a moment, then shook his head slowly. "Yes, I think the projector can handle two spools at once. I won't vouch for what it will look like, though."

He worked at the controls. The result was a chart that was neither black nor white, but a faded gray. The density of the chart was tremendously increased, filled as it was with nearly twice the number of stars and systems.

"A touch here," Karl Four murmured, "and we should see something interesting."

Twenty-odd points on the chart turned red. Spock studied them, then walked over and had a brief, tense conversation with the astronomer.

"The red glows indicate where two stars occupy the same space in both universes," he explained to the onlookers. "The difficulty is that while several are novas in our universe, none is sufficiently youthful to be birthing stars here.

"The star material here which will birth soonest, Karl Four tells me, is this point," and he indicated one of the pulsing lights. "It will spring to life in roughly three hundred fifty of our years . . . give or take a decade or two."

"And we haven't got three hundred fifty years—give or take anything," Kirk declared. "Though it's not a question of age." His mouth twisted slightly. "We'd all have returned to infancy and been long gone by then."

Spock inhaled deeply. "Unfortunately correct, Captain."

"There's the chance of keying one of these potential new novas into life here, gentlemen. Locate the best possible combination of swirling gases and concurrent pressure, and ignite the first thermonuclear reaction.

An overloaded ship engine could conceivably do it,"
Karl Four said.

"We thought of that," Kirk told him, "but we can't
use our warp-drive engines—that would leave us relatively helpless, our speed curtailed severely."

"How about one of our vessels?" the Arretian suggested.

"If you think it might work. I don't see us trying
anything else."

"There is one other problem." They turned to look
at Karla Five. "In order to avoid destruction, I had to
pass through the nova at maximum velocity. I understand that your vessel, Captain Kirk, is not capable of
such speeds."

"A good point, Captain," Spock agreed. "To which I
see no immediate solution."

"Of course, you're welcome to use my ship, Captain
Kirk. It is the most advanced of its type . . . we have
no others capable of reaching such speeds, either."

"Then I'm afraid that won't do us much good,
Karla," Kirk replied sadly. "Thanks for the offer . . .
but I have a crew of four hundred thirty, and your ship
is suitable for only a few people, at most."

"Captain," Spock said, suddenly brightening, "there
is a chance Karla Five's vessel *could* solve all these
problems. We require another, powerful vessel to go to
overload, to initiate the new star. We can use hers both
as an unmanned projectile, to accomplish this, and as a
tug to aid us in achieving the necessary speed. We need
merely keep our tractor beam attached. We gained the
velocity required to pass into this universe in this fashion. I do not see why we cannot use the same method
to pass out from it."

"Spock, you may be right. You'd better be, because
I don't see that we've got another choice," he finished
grimly.

"Of course, any miscalculation . . ." He paused
meaningfully. "If the reaction isn't sufficient to set off
the new star in this universe, we may run through a
murderous field of superhot plasma. Or if speed alone
is enough to carry us through, the proper distortion

may not be created. In that event, we could emerge right in the heart of an unstressed nova."

"In which case," April observed succinctly, "we won't have time to consider our mistake . . . having already ceased to exist."

Preparations proceeded smoothly, thanks to the aid of the sympathetic Arretians. Some of Arret's top physicists reworked the mathematics, to insure that everything would perform as required. For example, it was felt that merely overloading the extremely advanced engines which powered Karla Five's exploratory skiff would be insufficient to spark the necessary thermonuclear reaction in the center of the star-to-be. So the Arretian military loaded the smaller craft with compact but immensely powerful fusion weaponry, to provide a proper catalyst.

Linkages were established which would permit the *Enterprise*'s helm to control Karla Five's vessel as precisely as a living pilot could. Eventually, the two ships left Arretian orbit together, traveling at rapidly increasing speed and with the best wishes of Arret's scientific community. The prognosis was only slightly in favor of success, but both sides concealed their true feelings and concerns under a mask of empirical assurance.

"Captain's log, Stardate 5536.6," Kirk was reciting, days later. "Time continues to flow backward for us. We have set our course for a dead star aborning in this universe which corresponds to the nova Minerva in ours.

"There appears to be a new, correlating factor between the flow of time and our increasing speed, but as yet this has presented no difficulty. We are on course, and all instrumentation is operating at maximum efficiency, including the devices linking the *Enterprise* to the Arretian scout ship."

He concluded the entry and turned a gaze as yet only mildly concerned toward the science station. "Mr. Spock, any indication as to what the possible effects of the accelerated time-flow might be?"

"Theoretical only, thus far, Captain," his first officer

replied. Then he added the obvious, "Anyhow, we must proceed with the programmed course and velocity regardless of all side effects. It is our only chance."

Kirk nodded, looking over his shoulder, and smiled at the pacing figure of Commodore April. He had been walking his destinationless path ever since they had left Arret.

"You may as well relax, sir. As Mr. Spock says, our course of action is committed, unalterable. And that patch of brown in your hair is very becoming."

April stopped, grinned a lopsided grin at Kirk. "Thank you, Captain. You're looking rather on the youngish side yourself, lately. Don't let my aimless meandering worry you ... I *am* relaxing." The grin vanished, and he looked disappointedly at the deck.

"I have mixed feelings about the remainder of our journey, no matter what its outcome. Oh, I'll be glad to get home, all right, but not necessarily to Babel. That only means the official end of my career. Of my usefulness. . . ."

Kirk was spared the necessity of a reply as Spock broke in with an announcement. "I have visual contact with the region of the potential new star, Captain."

Kirk mentally thanked his first officer for the interruption—the conversation was beginning to make him uncomfortable. His tone turned businesslike.

"Let's see what we're heading into, Mr. Spock."

The *Enterprise*'s forward sensors leaped ahead, finally slowing to focus on still another rectangle of this fantastic, cream-colored universe with its black suns and feathery gray nebulae.

"I don't see anything, Mr. Spock."

"A moment, Captain. We are headed directly for it, but it is denser white matter in white space. I will superimpose an outline."

Adjustments at the science console produced a rough black circle in the center of the screen.

"If I didn't know better, Mr. Spock, I'd suspect it was another white hole."

"No, Captain, preliminary sensor readings indicate

it's nothing like the one we encountered near the Milky Way's Shapely Center.

"There is considerable stress, shifting gravitational potential, and other unusual phenomena present, but nowhere near the extreme distortions of the spatial matrix we encountered in the white hole."

"Just as well," Kirk murmured. "I've no desire to repeat that trip again." Uhura called over to him, cutting off his thoughts in midremembrance.

"Message coming in from Arret, Captain. Karla Five making contact."

"Put her through, Lieutenant."

Transmission all the way from Arret was no longer crystal-clear, but the resolution was sufficient to show the aged yet youthful scout standing before the starchart projector in her son's laboratory.

"I want to wish you luck, Captain Kirk," she said, her voice filtered and distorted with distance. "I was present at the official farewell, but I applied for and received permission to make this final broadcast. As I was, in a way, personally responsible for bringing you here, the government felt I was entitled to wish you on your way personally. The pity of it is that after all we've done, no matter what the astrophysicists tell me, I'll never know if you fail or succeed."

"Just keep in mind that you've done all you could for us, Karla," replied Kirk truthfully. "And perhaps you will know someday. Someday when a way is found of crossing the barriers between our universes in safety and comfort. When that day comes, we'll thank you personally for your help . . . in *our* universe, next time. The important thing is that you've shown such a journey is possible. We thank you also for the sacrifice of your vessel. You see, I know that your government couldn't force you to turn it over to us, and that you volunteered it freely."

"A small sacrifice, Captain," the fading, emotional voice declared. "The information I was able to bring back is worth more to my people than any number of such vessels. Indeed, the information your computer library supplied made up the loss of one scout many times over.

"I only hope that it proves to be a worthwhile sacrifice. Success to you, Captain Kirk, Mr. Spock, Commodore April, and all . . ."

The screen blanked. "Transmission ended from Arret, sir," Uhura reported dutifully.

"Thank you, Lieutenant. Mr. Spock?" The view of space forward resumed. "Mr. Sulu, how's the tractor link holding up?"

Sulu checked his read-outs. To ensure that the invisible bond joining the *Enterprise* and the smaller Arretian ship didn't break at a crucial juncture, every tractor beam on board that could be brought to bear was locked on the superfast scout.

"Still holding firm, Captain. The original tractor link as well as all subsequent holds."

"Very good, Lieutenant. Let me know immediately if the bonds show any sign of weakening."

Sulu nodded as Arex reported from navigation. "Speed increasing steadily, Captain. We're holding on course."

That left one last section to check. "Bridge to Engineering . . . Scotty, are you there?"

"Standin' by, Captain."

"What's our situation?"

"Stable so far, sir," the chief engineer reported. "Of course, I've some idea what to expect this time around, and we've prepared for it—I hope. That new bracin' installed by the Arretians seems to be doin' what they claimed it would. If it holds up under this passage it's goin' to cause some heavy thinking on the part of the engineers responsible for designin' warp-drive supports. Not to mention what a sensation those diagrams of that scout ship's engines are goin' to be."

"Don't get too excited about that, Scotty," Kirk reminded him. "Remember, the element that powers those engines is found only in the Arretian's universe. We'll have to work out the difficulties of interuniversal transport and travel before we can think of a cruiser traveling at warp-thirty or so."

"I know, Captain," Scott replied, trying not to sound as disappointed as he was. "Ah, but wouldn't it be a darlin' surprise for our friends the Klingons!"

It was hours later, when they had more than doubled their speed, that Kirk noticed the at once marvelous, ominous change creeping through the *Enterprise*.

He had been so involved in last-minute course calculations, in monitoring the status of the Arretian scout, that he had failed to see the startling alterations taking place all around him. In fairness, though, so had everyone else. The gradualness of the first changes—and their uniformity—were responsible for the oversight.

Metamorphosis was proceeding so rapidly now, however, that it struck Kirk like a blow to the belly. The subtle sensation that something was drastically different was concretized when McCoy and Sarah April reappeared on the bridge. The shift was most apparent in their faces.

The deep lines caused by too many patients lost through the unavailability of the necessary drugs, too many needless deaths incurred on hostile worlds, were missing from McCoy's visage. He was noticeably younger.

As was Dr. Sarah April, paragon of Starfleet medical technology, who was now a very unvenerable fortyish beauty devoid of white hair, lines around the eyes, and all other indications of advanced age.

Abruptly Kirk saw the bridge staff through clear eyes and a clear mind. Sulu and Uhura, he now noticed, had regained the appearance of teenagers. Spock showed the least amount of change, which was only natural as Vulcans aged more slowly than humans. It was hardest to tell when he looked at Arex, since adolescent Edoans often look exactly like their wizened elders.

"Mr. Spock, I think we have passed the point of needing theoretical opinions on the effects of the increased time-flow."

"I had noticed it before now, Captain," the first officer said somberly, "but as we have no alternative course of action, I saw no point in needlessly distressing anyone."

Kirk wasn't sure he agreed with Spock's reasoning, but he had no time to argue with it. He wasn't sure how much time he had left, period.

"I suppose the first crucial minute will be when our youngest crew member returns to . . . to the moment of birth," he ventured.

Spock concurred. "That will take place, taking into account a rapid increase in our regression corresponding to our increasing speed, in approximately eighteen minutes, thirty-five seconds, Captain. However, that will not be the *most* crucial time."

"Explain, Mr. Spock."

"Before that point is reached, we will all have returned to infantilism. And," he concluded, "this means we are losing our knowledge concomitant with our years, and both at an alarming rate. It is possible that we will be too young, mentally, to operate the *Enterprise* at the crucial stage in our interuniversal passage. . . ."

IV

Kirk pondered the problem for long minutes, then broke off when he found himself staring with a little too much fascination at the sixteen-year-old boy sitting before the now massive-looking helm console.

"How's our present course, Mr. Sulu?"

The youth started to reply, hesitated, and stared blankly at the now bewildering array of instrumentation spread before him. "I . . . I'm not sure," he finally confessed in a shockingly altered tenor. "What am I doing here, anyway? What are all these dials and gauges and lights?" He turned and stared with rising confusion at Kirk.

"And you . . . you're . . . ? Who are you, mister?"

"He's too young, Captain," Spock interrupted. "Far younger than he was when he entered Starfleet. Not only has he regressed beyond the point of knowing how to operate *Enterprise* instrumentation, his youthful mind is beginning to doubt its far larger store of memories. Look at Lieutenant Uhura."

Kirk turned and saw a puzzled young girl running her hands uncertainly over winking telltales.

"They are turning into children, Captain," Spock concluded.

"But they just can't lose all their acquired knowledge, Mr. Spock. Our physical makeup isn't the same as the Arretians."

"I suspect all the knowledge is still there, Captain," his first officer explained, "locked away deep within their minds. But the mechanism for retrieving such information is degenerating as they grow younger."

"We'll cope, somehow," countered Kirk tightly. "Mr. Arex, take over helm functions for Mr. Sulu. I want a full status report from all sections, Lieutenant Uhura. Lieutenant Uhura?"

"I beg your pardon, mister?" she replied dazedly.

"Never mind. Spock, you can fill in for her temporarily. Their replacements would only be as young and ineffective as they. You and Mr. Arex are the only longer-lived crew members on board."

"True, Captain," admitted Spock. "We will manage as long as we are able. But who will fill in for you?"

Kirk gave him a peculiar look. "What do you mean, 'fill in for me'?"

Spock explained patiently something Kirk knew but refused to believe. "You are a deal older than Lieutenant Sulu or Uhura, but at what age did you become a starship captain? How old were you when you entered Starfleet Academy? When did you take advanced navigation, or command mechanics?"

Kirk chewed that over, then finally nodded reluctant agreement. "We'll lose control rapidly, all right. By the time we reach the vicinity of the potential star, I'm not going to know what we have to do, let alone how to do it."

"As a Vulcan, I age the slowest, true," Spock commented. There was no hint of pride or racial arrogance in that statement. It was merely fact. Merely Spock. "I will be capable of retaining my effectiveness longer than anyone else.

"But I fear even I will become too young to know what to do at the crucial moment. It will be close . . . very close." He glanced at his controls, wondering idly at what moment they would become only glassed-in numbers for him. He wished he could divorce himself from his body to study the no doubt intriguing phenomenon at leisure.

"Ten minutes, fourteen seconds," he announced finally. "We may just make it, Captain, according to the final computer projection. At the appropriate moment it will be vital to activate the weaponry on board the Arretian scout. That must be handled by someone other than myself."

Kirk blinked at the strange words. He saw things plainly, but his thoughts were masked by thicker and thicker layers of uncertainty. Nothing related to anything else. He found he could describe but not explain, see without understanding, perceive but not evaluate.

Children surrounded him, at the helm, at Communications. And at the navigation console, even Arex was beginning to look decidedly cuddly.

"Captain," a demanding voice said, "do you think you will be able to handle the Arretian engine overload functions?"

"Overload . . . engine overload? How do we do that, Mr. Spock?"

The first officer inhaled deeply. In his still-exacting mind, their chances dropped a few percentage points. "I fear I must assume control, Captain. You are no longer able to command the *Enterprise*."

Kirk retained enough maturity to readily agree. "Whatever you say, Spock. What shall I do?"

A new voice spoke up. Its master had just now appeared on the bridge, had only taken stock of the recent developments.

He was tall, straight, supremely confident. The voice was new and at the same time familiar. A bit softer now, perhaps, its timbre sharp and precise. Kirk thought he recognized it, thought he recognized the stranger as well.

"I'm sorry, Mr. Spock," the voice said commandingly. "As long as I'm aboard, I'm still senior officer here. My subsequent appointment as ambassador-at-large does not supersede my Starfleet ranking, it only complements it. I hate to pull rank, but I'd guess that in another five minutes even you will become incapable of command, much less of performing intricate operations." He checked his madly revolving watch, noting the speed with which the hands were spinning in reverse.

"That's not soon enough to execute the few but vital maneuvers essential to our hope of return."

Spock did not argue; there was no reason to. The commodore's logic was unassailable. "You are correct, of course, Commodore April. I had forgotten all but regular crew under the stress of the moment. I would be grateful if you would assume command."

"I hereby do so officially, Mr. Spock." He sounded slightly bemused now. "But why the 'commodore'? It's Captain . . . Captain April."

"Who?" muttered Spock.

"Bob . . . ?"

The young commodore-captain turned.

"We seem to be the only adults left on the bridge," Sarah April observed. "They're all children now, or teenaged."

Her husband nodded. "Make sure they don't hurt themselves, Sarah." He turned his attention to the instruments at the helm. "If we're going to go home, instead of to blazes, we have to ignite this star at just the right moment. Mr. Spock, I realize your reasoning powers are now impaired, but how are you at still following orders?"

Spock strained visibly. "Information . . . is vanishing rapidly, sir. For the moment . . . yes, I can function. The sensation is somewhat akin to submitting to anesthesia."

"Right. Assume the navigator's position." The adolescent Vulcan proceeded to do so, gently moving a squawking, feathered protester out of the chair.

"Report, Mr. Spock," April said from the helm.

"The potential star is directly ahead, Captain." The first officer's manner and inflection were steady as ever. Only a close acquaintance would have noted the lighter, slightly less serious tone in his speech. "Bearing, mark," and he strenuously recited the readings, unsure of their meaning. But observation did not require as much knowledge as interpretation, and another pair of eyes was what April needed now.

"Activate the weaponry on board the Arretian ship."

That almost . . . almost defeated Spock. Knowledge was draining from him like water from a cracked pitcher. It took a long minute of painful thought before he was able to key the relatively simple command required to arm the awesome energies packed into the tiny scout.

"Activated, Captain," he finally acknowledged.

"Nine seconds to ignition," April recited, staring at

the helm readouts. "Seven, six . . ." His gaze rose to the main screen, as did Sarah April's and Spock's.

A black flower blossomed before them, its stretching petals tinged with violet and royal blue. The unnatural colors were startling against the pure white background of space.

April spared a split second for a survey of the bridge. No longer did it resemble the hub of one of the Federation's most storied, most efficient ships. Instead it had taken on the appearance of an undisciplined interspecies nursery.

Children and in some cases infants now babbled and struggled within the confines of baggy clothing grown monstrously large for their tiny forms: Naturally, the inorganic materials had not shrunk along with the crew members. If anything, April noted with alarm, the rate of reverse was accelerating. Surely the first officer now fumbling confusedly at the navigation console was no older than seven. He was past following even simple commands.

There was, however, still one other person on the bridge who could perform the remaining crucial maneuvers. One whose ability matched if not exceeded his own. He looked over his shoulder at the radiantly beautiful woman watching him.

"Sarah, do you remember any of your basic navigation?"

"Like it was yesterday, Bob." She moved to the navigation console while the commodore-captain assumed the command chair.

"Keep us on course, whatever else happens, whatever might happen to me," April told her. She studied the instrumentation briefly, moved her hands over the dials and switches. It seemed like only yesterday she was tested on similar boards to pass her basic command functions classes at the Academy.

A small adjustment was called for here. The computer identified the deviation and brought it to the attention of its human masters. It could do no more. It needed an organic mind to order the necessary shift in course. Sarah April moved almost automatically to provide that command.

Satisfied, the navigation computer realigned the *Enterprise*. Once more it was on the course prescribed for its eventual salvation . . . or destruction.

Tail first, the great cruiser plunged into the center of a rapidly heating mass of pressurized gases and particles. The tremendous release of energy produced by the volatized Arretian ship had kindled strange reactions among the mass of already unstable material.

As a tremendous shaking suddenly gripped the *Enterprise*, fusion began.

Sarah April felt like a pebble in a tin can as she clung tightly to the navigation console. But Commodore-Captain April locked himself into the command chair and exulted in the glory conveyed by the main viewscreen.

For what seemed like hours, but was mere seconds, they rode the shock wave of ruptured space.

Abruptly, without warning, the buffeting ceased. There was only the soft hum of monitors, the quiet beeps and mutters of unstressed instruments.

April became aware that he was still frozen to his seat. Slowly he relaxed his muscles, let his body slump. He became aware of something else: His eyes were closed tight enough to hurt.

He opened them slowly, and as usual his eyes registered the view forward before his mind comprehended.

Black space flecked with colored suns.

They were home again.

Sarah April left the navigation console and moved slowly to his side. "The computer can hold us steady here. I didn't have enough navigation to be able to reprogram us from wherever we are, Bob. That may be a problem."

She nodded to where the seven-year-old Spock was sitting near the navigation station, staring back at them with precocious, wide eyes.

April's attention was still focused on the screen. "I never thought pure blackness could look so lovely." Finally he looked away, down, and embraced her as hard as he had the rocking command chair only moments before.

"We did it. We're back in our own universe again," he finally sighed, releasing her. Now he could turn his attention to Spock and the rest of the ship's youthful crew.

"The reverse aging process seems to have stopped, but I see no signs of rapid aging beginning. The effect apparently operates only in the negative universe."

"Does that mean they're all going to remain children?" Sarah asked.

"No . . . no, that doesn't make sense, either," he said thoughtfully. He gestured at Spock, who amiably gestured back. "I have no doubt that Spock, Captain Kirk, and the others will return to their normal ages naturally —but at our universe's normal speed.

"That would mean, for example, that Mr. Spock will have to grow up all over again. Unless . . ."

"The transporter records!" Dr. April exclaimed. "It retains the records of their original molecular structure. It *could* return them to the age they were when they last transported."

"It could," he agreed. "But the entire ship's crew . . . it will take some time. We're going to be busy for a while, my love."

"You think it will work, too, Bob?" She appeared uncertain now. "Hasn't it been tried before, and found not to? I seem to recall experiments. If it worked, everyone could have near immortality, simply by having their youthful selves recorded for transporting and then, upon aging, entering transporters to be reintegrated according to their preserved youthful records."

"Yes to everything you said, Sarah," April concurred. "But one exception should—*has* to—make a difference. Remember, the molecular structure of everyone on board has been altered by unnatural, extrauniversal forces. Those fountain-of-youth experiments with transporters weren't carried out on people who'd been exposed to the accelerated time-flow and radiations and who-knows-what of the negative universe.

"It's those molecular changes that should be reversible, Sarah. At least, the theory seems sound, if I remember my transporter mechanics correctly." He smiled. "As you say, it seems like yesterday. But we don't have to use the transporter, Sarah. We can remain young, live our lives over again. To be able to do that, have a second life—it was worth the trip to the negative universe and the difficulties of returning. We've found a true fountain of youth, Sarah—in mathematics and spatial physics, instead of an obscure plot of mythical topography."

"And all anyone has to do to make use of it," she said sadly, "is to have a great amount of daring and a ship that can travel at warp-thirty-five. I'm afraid that our experience is going to prove unique."

"I'm afraid you're right, Sarah. Actually, we're not going to live our lives over again, are we? We're going to live a second life. That's good." He smiled, warm, loving, a together-understanding smile. "I wouldn't want to live the other one over again. I don't see how we could ever improve on what we've had already. No, Sarah, we've been blessed beyond any other people, been granted a special privilege. We musn't abuse it."

"We didn't abuse it the first time around, Bob. I'm not at all worried about a repeat performance."

April's theory about the action of negative-universe forces turned out to be correct. They started with the bridge crew, and breathed sighs of relief when the adult analogs reappeared to take the place of the children who had entered the transporter.

Each member of the crew exited from the alcove with a splitting headache. This was the only noticeable side effect—headache, and a uniform sometimes badly askew. Both ailments were easily treated.

It was slow going at first, carefully reprogramming according to old records and then reintegrating with equal care. But once the engineering officers had been brought back to true maturity, they were able to take over the task and proceed with greater speed and efficiency.

So it didn't take overlong for the *Enterprise* to return to normal strength, experientially as well as in numbers.

Kirk leaned back in the command chair and reflected on his brief but profound reentry into childhood. Everyone on board had reacted differently to the experience, and not a few were undergoing psychiatric outpatient treatment for traumas incurred as a result.

"I don't think we have any serious cases, Jim," McCoy had informed him. "But if you see any of the younger ensigns walking around sucking their thumbs, try not to be too harsh on them."

Once again it was McCoy whose easy humor had shattered a tense, potentially nerve-racking situation. Any lingering worries among the crew vanished in laughter as the good doctor's comment passed around the ship.

Most of the experience had faded to the memory of a distant dream for Kirk, but there was one resurrected bit of personal history that had stuck with him.

He had a picture of a small, feisty boy in preschool, with the instructor hovering over his computer terminal, bawling him out for running mock battles with the math keys instead of practicing computation tables.

"Jimmy Kirk, I've told you and told you," she scolded. "If you keep wasting your time with such nonsense you'll never amount to anything!"

"Something amusing, Captain Kirk?"

"Hmmm ... what?" Kirk started, then glanced back and up at a youthful Robert April. "No, Commodore, I was just thinking that among your other numerous distinctions, you're now going to be regarded as the youngest commodore in the fleet. But of course, you're not. Let's see, extrapolating from your present recorded age, as opposed to your new actual one, I'd estimate that you can probably retire at the natural age of one hundred and thirty. That should give you over a hundred years in the service, Commodore.

"I'd give a lot to see what Starfleet accounting's going to do with *those* figures! Either they'll have to refigure the basis for computing pensions, or else you can retire tomorrow with a full commodore's pension and a whole lifetime to enjoy it in."

"There is a host of fascinating ramifications, Captain," April agreed. "But as you can guess, financial considerations are not foremost in my mind." He looked downcast.

"The Minerva Nova's not far from Babel. And we'll be there shortly. I know that should make me happy, Jim, but it doesn't any more. I don't care much about money." He looked up, and his sorrowful eyes bore into Kirk's own, the same light of deep space glowing in their depths.

"You, of all people, can understand what does."

Under pressure of that pleading stare, Kirk couldn't hold back any longer.

"Well then, I might as well tell you that we've been in contact with Starfleet ever since we regained control of the *Enterprise*. Naturally, they were most interested in the details of our journey into the negative universe. *All* the details, Commodore."

April looked at him unsurely. There was something in the captain's voice. "What do you mean, Jim?"

"Nothing . . . just that we received a reply from Starfleet headquarters, relayed all the way to us, which might cheer you up a bit. I'd intended waiting to reveal its contents until we were in orbit around Babel, but"—he shrugged—"I couldn't stand to see a young man cry.

"Lieutenant Uhura, would you repeat the message to Commodore and Dr. April?"

Uhura nodded happily. Like everyone else on board, she had come to regard the Aprils as fellow crew members rather than as distinguished passengers. So it gave her pleasure equal to Kirk's own to be able to read, "In view of Commodore Robert April's heroic actions aboard the U.S.S. *Enterprise* this stardate, the senior command is reviewing mandatory retirement regulations with special regard to the unusual circumstances surrounding Commodore April's present physical status.

"His earlier requests to remain in active service will

be given priority reevaluation. End communiqué." She looked back across the bridge and smiled.

April said nothing, but Sarah's left hand slid smoothly into his right. His palm enveloped hers as naturally and reassuringly as a snowbank settles around a sleeping sled-dog.

"And I have more time to continue my research," she murmured. "Perhaps this time I can accomplish one or two things."

"Well, bravo," April finally exclaimed confidently. "Maybe now I can talk them into doing away with that idiot mandatory retirement age altogether." His voice rose with the zeal of renewed youth.

"Retirement shouldn't be a function of abstract statistics. By God, the Federation's got to realize that a person's ability isn't automatically invalidated on a specific date."

"I'll support you on that, Bob," Kirk agreed, "and would even if I didn't see myself repeating your complaint a number of years from now."

"Insertion into Babel orbit in one hour fifteen minutes, Captain," Sulu reported from the helm. April looked resigned.

"Sarah and I had better get our things together, Jim. I may have to have some emergency alterations performed on my dress uniform."

"And I can't wait to perform some on *mine*," Dr. April added vivaciously.

April half-whispered the next words, but Kirk heard them clearly. "And, Jim, even if it wasn't too pleasant for the rest of you, thanks for the opportunity to be a starship captain again."

They turned to leave the bridge, and as they did so Kirk noticed that Sarah April was holding the brilliant, revived Capellan flower.

"Bob always did say that the *Enterprise* had the best crew in Starfleet. I see it's as true today as it was thirty years ago. Thank you for everything, Captain Kirk."

"Doctor April," he acknowledged softly. Then his tone brightened. "I always wanted to be a kid again. After having the chance, I can see I wasn't missing much." He gestured at the blossom. "I see your flower's bloomed again."

She was staring up at the contented face of the commodore, but she heard him. "Everything has, Captain," she murmured.

Kirk watched them until they had left the bridge. He turned and settled back into the chair. There was still a little time left before he would have to go through the rigors of donning a full-dress uniform and making inane conversation with boring but important people.

For now he could spend a number of pleasant hours doing nothing but staring at the exhilarating, lush blackness of the *real* universe.

As they neared Babel, he noticed Spock staring into apparent nothingness. Such abstract concentration was not unusual for the first officer, however. Often his thoughts were his own best friend. But Kirk detected a hint of a peculiar expression crossing Spock's face from time to time.

Idly, he asked, "What did you think of your temporary return to the joys of childhood, Spock? You didn't age down to a squalling babe like most of us, so your memory of those minutes is probably stronger."

"Joys of childhood, Captain?" the first officer echoed diffidently. He assumed a firm, no-nonsense tone. "Childhood is a time of indiscipline, insecurity, and instability, both emotional and logical. From a physiological and informational point of view the experience was somewhat intriguing, but it was otherwise nonbeneficial. I would hardly call it a 'joy,' and I surely have no special desire to repeat it."

"Naturally, of course," Kirk muttered, taken a bit aback by his friend's logical appraisal of what, for him, had been a warm if confusing experience. "I suppose I agree with you. After all, that's the only rational way to look at it."

"Quite."

"By the way, what were you thinking of just now?"

"Captain?"

"A moment ago. You were wandering."

"I was . . . analyzing the experience in question and culling its scientific values."

Kirk seemed disappointed. "Of course, though it almost appeared once that you might have been talking to yourself."

"A not impossible phenomenon, Captain. I am not immune to subliminal vocalizations. It is merely rare in Vulcans. But I am interested. What did you think you heard?"

"Nothing that made sense," the Captain replied, repeating it slowly. "Ee-chiya—that's all."

"You are correct, Captain, nothing that makes sense." He returned his attention to his multitude of instruments, his readouts and gauges and illumined lists of scientific minutiae.

"It vaguely resembled an obscure Vulcan scientific term, nothing more. Nothing more. . . ."

The astounding metamorphosis of the Aprils was the highlight of the ambassadorial gathering at Babel. Expecting to honor an aged, white-haired couple, the conferees were shocked when the youthful pair presented themselves at function after stunned function.

All they met were shocked, stunned, and envious. Hopes did not fall even when inquiries into the transformation by friends old and new revealed the methodology necessary to achieve the radical alteration. None present regarded the dangers of diving into a nova seriously—old men have nothing to lose. It made some of them bolder than the rawest recruit.

The devolution of the Aprils would have one side effect. It would speed, with the aid of the charts provided by Arretian scientists, research into warp-drive technology.

Now immortality had become a question of getting rapidly from place to place, in order to get from time to time . . .

V

As it turned out, Kirk was spared the enervating agony of attending endless speeches, parties, and conferences. A Federation cruiser not on planned layover could not be permitted to languish unengaged at an idle port of call. Their job had been to deliver Commodore April - and his wife to the conference. This done, it was only a matter of time before new orders were received.

Kirk kept a reluctant smile on his face as he took leave of various representatives on Babel.

"Emergency priority signal received aboard, Captain," Spock whispered to him. Kirk frowned, then reapplied the reluctant smile he had been artfully employing all afternoon.

"Sorry to have to run, Ambassador Werthel, Admiral M'aart, Dame M'arrt," he explained hastily to the little group. "Duty runs on its own timetable."

"Arr, yes," the ample mate of the Caitian admiral purred in remembrance. "How clearrly I myself rrememberr the time only a few yearrs ago when—"

"Yes, well, you'll have to tell me all about it, in full detail, the next time we can get together," Kirk assured her, backing smoothly toward the doorway. "Let's get out of here, Mr. Spock," he said feelingly, "before this smile cracks my face."

"A physiological impossibility, Captain, though the meaning is clear."

With mixed feelings Kirk reentered the bridge: relief at the return to comfortable surroundings (how that admiral's wife could whine!), but apprehension at what would prompt Starfleet to break in on a diplomatic conference.

"You're certain this was an emergency priority call, Lieutenant?" he asked Uhura.

"Yes, sir. I keyed the proper response code the moment I heard that you and Mr. Spock were back on board. The message should be coming through any second."

"All right, Lieutenant." Tap, tap, click, tap ... He forced his fingers to freeze on the command-chair armrest, forced himself to listen to the quiet. "Mr. Spock, has the science section noted anything out of the ordinary in this region?"

"Negative, Captain. I ran a standard query through all subsections the moment I arrived back on board. Everything in this sector reports in normal and undisturbed."

"Call coming through, Captain."

"Um. Put it on the main screen, Lieutenant."

Kirk swiveled slightly as the screen cleared. Crisp with power, it showed the slight form of an aged Oriental seated behind a gleaming chrome desk devoid of ornamentation. Long white shoulder-length hair was combed straight back, and the creases in that young-old face seemed as fresh and as neatly cut as the lines of her uniform. Only the eyes of polished hazel revealed an intensity inspired by something other than age. They hinted at heavy burdens borne by generations. Only in the last few had those burdens changed from physical to mental.

A hand came up in casual, knowing wave. Three stripes decorated the sleeve.

"Greetings, Captain Kirk," a surprisingly strong voice said over the speakers and across parsecs.

Kirk's reply was one of respectful surprise. This he hadn't expected. "Hello, Commodore Sen. How are things at Starfleet Security?"

The commodore smiled wistfully. "Interesting, as always, Captain Kirk. Interesting and perpetually worrisome. And, as always, people rather than events cause the most trouble. For example, how do the names Van and Char Delminnen strike you?"

"At a vague angle, Commodore. Sorry, but I—"

"Excuse me, Captain, but I believe I am familiar with the persons in question. If memory serves me—"

"Doesn't it always?" Uhura murmured. Spock favored her with a mildly reproving glance.

"If memory serves, Van Delminnen was a Fellow of the London Institute for Theoretical Physics some years ago. A research Fellow. His specialty lay on the fringe of what was known about the specific gravity of heavy elements.

"Apparently his brilliance was exceeded only by his unorthodox methodology, which was in turn matched by the volatility of his temperament. He withdrew from the institute amid a storm of accusations and counteraccusations. Dropped from sight . . . I recall the tape well."

"Nothing heard of them since?"

"The only information I have encountered, Captain, were rumors that he and his sister were living on an otherwise uninhabited moon in the Theta Draconis system."

"Your opinion of him . . . from the information you've encountered?"

The first officer paused thoughtfully for a moment. "Arrogant and harmless . . . a crippled genius, Captain, possibly mentally unstable."

"You are partially correct, First Officer Spock," the serious voice called from the screen. "Brilliant—decidedly. Unorthodox—yes. Mentally unstable . . . perhaps. But we have reason to doubt the 'harmless.' " She reached off-screen and consulted several sheets of plastic. After a cursory glance, she turned back to the visual pickup.

"Captain Kirk, a prospecting vessel whose specialty is searching out marginal deposits of valuable metals passed through the limits of the Theta Draconis system ten standard days ago. They were returning to mine a small deposit of polonium reported by the original drone survey of the system as existing on a continent of the ninth planet." She leaned forward.

"Instead of the ninth world, they found a previously unreported asteroid cluster of considerable mass. A similar cluster had also taken the place of the system's eighth planetary body. Simple calculations by the ship's computer indicated what you must already have suspected: The mass of the two asteroidal groupings very nearly equaled that of the two missing worlds.

"As you might imagine, they left the system without pursuing these unusual developments more closely, straining their engines to their limits.

"I am. told," she continued, as the bridge crew listened in amazement, "that normal spatial phenomena can in no way account for this dual disaster. We must therefore assume that abnormal forces are at work. Combine this information with the detection of highly unusual, very powerful radiation emanating from the system's largest moon, which circles its fifth world— well, I hardly think I need to draw you a diagram, Captain Kirk.

"You see, Mr. Spock, the rumors were correct. The Delminnens have taken up residence in the Theta Draconis system. They have also seemingly taken to making small planetoids out of big planets.

"Starfleet is very worried. *I* am very worried. And since the *Enterprise* is the Federation ship nearest the Theta Draconis system, you too should be worried, Captain Kirk.

"You will proceed immediately to the system in question and establish contact with the Delminnens. You will invite Van Delminnen to return to Terra, where he is to be granted a permanent appointment to Starfleet Research at a generous annual stipend."

"Suppose," Kirk ventured, "Delminnen declines our invitation? He has no reason to hold any love for Federation institutions."

"In that unfortunate event," the commodore replied, "you are authorized to utilize whatever means you deem necessary to entice him and his sister aboard ship. Good luck, Captain Kirk."

The image vanished. "Transmission concluded, Captain," Uhura reported. "Standard recording procedures were in operation."

"Thank you, Lieutenant. I want that blanket authorization made part of the formal record." He turned to his first officer. "Mr. Spock . . . opinions?"

"A device capable of producing the effect described by the commodore seems beyond the capability of modern technology, Captain. Total annihilation of a planetary mass, yes. Selective disintegration, no."

"And yet it appears that Delminnen can do just that. No wonder Starfleet is concerned." Kirk turned to the helm. "Mr. Sulu, set course for Theta Draconis Five. Warp-five. Mr. Arex, sound yellow alert. All stations will remain on same until the Delminnens are secured on board."

"You make those two sound like a dangerous weapon, Captain," Sulu observed solemnly.

"That's exactly how the commodore described them, Lieutenant. And that's exactly how we're going to treat them—at least until we find out what's been going on in the Draconis system . . ."

Great bands of orange, red, and yellow turned Theta Draconis Five into a monstrous ball of poisoned softness. Its hostile surface lay swathed in a fuzzy cloak of ammonia and methane, and it howled at the ether with wild, undisciplined radiations.

Records indicated that it was attended by seven satellites, one of which the *Enterprise* was currently orbiting. It was not the largest or the smallest, but it was surely unique, for it possessed a breathable atmosphere.

". . . and little else," Spock intoned, his eyes fixed to the gooseneck viewer. "Other than the livable atmosphere, there is nothing of interest on the moon, nothing to make it attractive to settlers. It has neither commercial nor military value."

"All of which makes it ideal for a would-be hermit like Delminnen," Kirk observed as he stared at the rust-colored globe and its startlingly white miniature icecaps. He touched a switch on the command-chair arm.

"Captain's log, Stardate 5536.8. We have arrived at Theta Draconis and established orbit around the habitable moon of the fifth planet, where we are hoping to encounter the elusive Delminnens and their mysterious weapon . . . if indeed it is a weapon, if it indeed exists.

"Personally, I am skeptical as to the existence of said device. But Mr. Spock has verified the appearance of two unreported asteroid clusters in the positions formerly occupied by planets eight and nine, so some immensely powerful force *has* been at work in this system." The captain closed down the log and looked to his left. "Initial report, Mr. Spock?"

The first officer looked across, his attention turned from his readouts. "Mostly desert, tundra or hot, with little free water. No indication of life more developed than the lower invertebrates. It's easy to see why the Delminnens selected this particular satellite. It offers nothing of interest to the most bored traveler."

"Then perhaps they won't mind leaving it so much. Lieutenant Uhura, see if you can raise the Delminnens. Try near the edge of the north polar cap—that appears to be the most hospitable section of this moon."

"Aye, sir." She turned to her instrumentation and responded after a surprisingly short pause. "Captain, I have made some kind of aural-visual contact already."

"They must have some detection equipment, then," Kirk noted. "Very well, flash the image on the main screen." He threw Spock a quick glance. "Get a fix on the transmitter's location and relay it to Transporter Control."

Spock moved to comply as Uhura struggled with her equipment. "The signal is weak but clear . . . there."

The figure that appeared was that of a shockingly young man: rail-thin, pale-skinned, with too-large eyes bordering a shark-hook of a nose. Straight sandy hair fell in hirsute drips across his face, and he brushed constantly, nervously at the strands.

"Who the devil are you and what do you want?"

Spock had moved to stand next to the command chair. "Sociable fellow, isn't he?" Kirk whispered to him, before turning to the screen and assuming his most pleasant tone.

"Good day to you, Professor Delminnen. I am James Kirk, Captain of the starship *Enterprise*, currently in orbit around your charming worldlet. I come at the urgent request of Starfleet Command."

"I'll bet." Delminnen smirked, smiling at some private joke.

"I have been instructed to offer you, in the name of the Federation, a permanent research position in advanced physical theory at the Starfleet Institute itself, with all the honors thereunto attached." He kept a straight face as he added, "There has been considerable renewed interest in some of your early theories, you see."

And the later developments, Kirk added, but to himself only.

"May I have the pleasure of conveying your acceptance to Starfleet headquarters?"

"Just . . . just a minute, Captain," Delminnen said. "I need a moment to consider."

Those aboard the *Enterprise* waited while the figure disappeared from the screen. The lift doors slid apart, and Dr. McCoy entered the bridge. He looked from the now blank screen to Kirk. The captain put a finger to his lips as Delminnen reappeared.

"I have considered your words, Captain Kirk," he said, "and find I don't believe a one of them." His voice rose angrily. "Why should those scientific cretins at Starfleet suddenly have the desire, or the sense, to request my services? Why should they now wish to subject me to honor instead of ridicule?"

Kirk took a deep breath. "I think you know the answer to that, Delminnen. Evidence of your . . . experimentation in this system has reached command levels. Naturally, everyone is anxious to admire the development which—"

"I thought as much," Delminnen said. His smirk turned into a wide, unfriendly smile. "I just wanted to hear it out loud. *Admire* pagh! They want to steal my knowledge! They always take what they can't understand." He all but snarled into the pickup.

"You can tell those mathematical morons what they can do with their honors, Captain. And if you don't leave me and my sister alone, you'll find yourself the recipient of a demonstration of just how *admirable* my work here is."

Kirk stared quietly at the suddenly blank screen. "So much," he murmured softly, "for diplomacy. What do you think of our reluctant guest, Mr. Spock?"

The first officer considered. "A difficult speciman. I can understand how such a psychological type could produce peculiar theories, but it eludes me completely as to how he could translate those theories into anything practical. Yet it seems he has. We must handle him the same way one would store a photon torpedo with a sensitive detonator—forcefully but with great care."

"I concur. Order a security landing party to stand by in the Main Transporter Room."

"Armed, Captain?"

"Armed."

Spock rose and turned to leave, adding, "Then I think it best that I instruct those chosen myself, so that everyone is fully cognizant of the difficulties involved."

As the lift doors closed behind the science officer, Kirk turned to the still-silent McCoy. "What's your professional opinion of Delminnen, Bones?"

"You mean, does he appear sane?"

Kirk gave a twisted smile. "Nothing so obvious. What I want to know is . . . is he sane enough? Or is he likely to go off the deep end when we knock on his front door and ask him to accompany us?"

"Well, he's arrogant, suspicious, and possibly a borderline paranoid, but I don't think he's homicidal, Jim. And his arrogance is rather reassuring."

Kirk frowned in puzzlement.

"He's too certain of his own importance to be suicidal," McCoy explained.

"I hope you're right. In any case, you'll have an opportunity to make a firsthand diagnosis any minute. You're coming down with Spock and me."

"Me? What for?"

"Our orders say to utilize all necessary means to bring Delminnen and his sister back with us. If he becomes violent and we have to be less than tactful with him, I want you along to pick up the pieces." Kirk pushed against the arms of the chair and sighed resignedly. "Let's get it over with."

"Captain!"

Kirk turned from the lift to look sharply back at the helm. "What is it, Mr. Sulu?"

The helmsman was working hastily with a bank of instruments that had been silent the entire journey from Babel. They were all suddenly active.

"Detectors indicate another vessel emerging from the planet's shadow."

Kirk rushed back to his seat. "Identification?"

"Not possible yet."

"Mr. Arex, have you a fix on her?"

"Yes, Captain," came the gentle, whistling reply. "It is a capital ship, apparently non-Federation in origin."

"Full magnification on the forward scanners, Mr. Sulu."

The screen lit up, giving a view of the slowly turning gas giant. Suddenly the intruder seemed to leap forward, to show an irregular, though clearly artificial, shape outlined against the brilliant hues of the planet's dense atmosphere.

"That's a Klingon cruiser, Jim," McCoy declared.

"I can see that, Bones," Kirk muttered. "Mr. Sulu, sound red alert. Mr. Arex, align phasers to—"

"Receiving transmission from the Klingon ship, Captain," Uhura interrupted.

"Acknowledge their signal, Lieutenant." He turned an expectant gaze to the viewscreen.

The Klingon who appeared there was seated in his counterpart of Kirk's command chair, but his height was evident nonetheless. His attitude was one of relaxed attention—in fact, he very nearly slouched. Except for the tight set of his lips and the churning one might detect beneath unusually bushy brows, he appeared almost friendly. And when the image had fully resolved at both ends of the transmission, he even smiled.

"Well, well . . . it is true what is said about the false

size of the universe. I have been expecting and dreading such a meeting for many years.

"How have you been, Jim?"

A soft sigh of air on the bridge came as several jaws dropped simultaneously.

"He called you 'Jim,' " McCoy finally whispered in astonishment. "You two *know* each other?" But Kirk continued to stare at the screen, ignoring the question.

"Hello, Kumara. It *is* you?"

"It is indeed none other, old friend. A strange place, after so many years, for a reunion, is it not?"

"Jim!" McCoy was fairly dancing with curiosity.

"Not now, Bones," Kirk replied firmly. His voice rose as he addressed the attentive figure on the screen. "Yes, it's a strange place for a reunion, Commander . . . it is 'Commander' now, isn't it?"

The figure smiled again and nodded.

"In fact, it's such a strange place that I wonder what you're doing here. This system is far off Imperial patrol routes."

The Klingon commander shifted in his seat. "A reasonable question, Jim. One which I might equally well ask of you. But since you inquired first . . . I have been instructed by the Imperial Resources Bureau to survey this system with regard to locating salvageable resources. While I will concede its greater proximity to the Federation sphere, you will recognize that it has not been formally claimed by your government. Therefore, we have as much right here as you.

"You are welcome to whatever you may find, though. With the slight exception of the sun-forsaken bit of sand you now orbit, our explorations have proven singularly unprofitable. There is practically nothing here worthy of Imperial attention . . . doubly true when one considers the distance to the nearest Imperial world.

"But enough of business!" The smile widened. "It is good to see you again, Jim. I invite you to share a container of Gellian *vitz* with me. Would you do me the honor of joining me aboard, say, ten of your minutes from now? Or, if you prefer, I can come aboard the *Enterprise*."

Kirk smiled in return. "No, your ship will be fine. The honor is mine, Kumara. I accept."

"I am gratified. Till then . . ."

Kirk's smile held until the Klingon commander's image had vanished. His expression turned grim, and he snapped at the chair pickup.

"Transporter Room—stand by to transport landing party. Mr. Spock?"

"Here, Captain," the reply came.

"Red alert was sounded because there's a Klingon cruiser in the area. All personnel are to transport down with one hand on their sidearms."

"Very good, Captain."

Kirk clicked off, and McCoy had to run to reach the elevator with him. "Why the rush, Jim? You can't possibly expect to get Delminnen and his sister off-moon in time to make your appointment with this Kumara."

Kirk's tone was low, curt. "Listen, Bones, Kumara may just be the best starship commander the Klingons have. You can bet your precision nerve welder the Emperor didn't send him this far from base to play prospector! I'll also bet that hypothetical bottle of Gellian *vitz* he mentioned that he's here because Klingon intelligence got wind of that Federation prospector's report. They're prospecting, all right—and if they get their hands on Delminnen, they'll mine him for all he's worth and they won't be too concerned about putting him back together when they've finished with him."

McCoy hesitated momentarily. "Jim, I asked you if you knew this Kumara . . . personally, I meant. You waved me off. Where do you know each other from so well that you immediately call each other by first names?"

"Is it that important, Bones?"

"Well, now, I don't know, Jim," McCoy said evenly. "When two enemy captains display a certain degree of familiarity unheard of in previous—"

"All right," Kirk broke in, turning to face the doctor. "Yes, Kumara and I know each other on an informal basis. Did you ever hear of the FEA, Bones?"

McCoy considered. "No . . . no, wait a second. The Friendship Exchange Action, wasn't it?"

Kirk nodded. "Remember what it was about?"

"Sure—it was well documented in all the psychology journals. Was set up during one of those brief friendly periods between the Federation and the Klingon Empire. Some bright medical theorist thought it might promote understanding between peoples if academy cadets from both cultures spent some time in close contact with one another. The program was limited to command candidates, if I remember right."

"It was and you do," Kirk acknowledged as the lift doors slid apart.

"Do what?" Spock inquired politely, and Kirk was forced to explain as he and McCoy entered the Transporter Room.

"Gentlemen, Kumara is one of the sharpest, smartest individuals I've ever met, and we can be thankful the Empire hasn't another dozen like him. He's also the only Klingon I've encountered who wasn't so puffed up with his own importance that he ignored his opponent's capabilities. And he expects us to believe he's here for casual 'exploration'!"

"Begging your pardon, Captain," Spock commented, "but this still doesn't explain how you come to address each other in so familiar a fashion."

"Oh, that. We were roommates, Mr. Spock." He led them into the transporter alcove.

Five armed crew members were already there, each standing at the ready on his respective disk. One small, dark-skinned man saluted as the three officers stepped up into the alcove.

"Ensign Gemas and landing party reporting ready, sir."

"Very good, Ensign." Kirk looked at the waiting group. "We may have to move fast . . . be prepared for anything."

Short, confident nods; a few muffled "ayes."

Kirk turned to face the console. "Scotty, I want you

to stay with us at all times. Keep the transporter energized. If I'm right about our obliging visitor, we may
have to come aboard in a hurry."

"No need to worry, Captain. I'm not movin' until
you're all back right where you are now."

"Good. Try to set us down about fifty meters from
the surface transmitter coordinates . . . in some cover,
if information is sufficient to permit it."

Scotty manipulated the instrumentation, and Kirk
saw him waver and disappear. He wondered if an
armed Klingon would replace the tense figure of his
chief engineer.

The security-team members were already drawing
their phasers as they materialized. They landed light-
footed, owing to the weak gravity, breathing short and
fast in the thin air. A few stars shone through the violet sky, and the immense globe of Theta Draconis
Five hung like a baleful candy eye above the far horizon.

A few scraggly, ground-hugging shreds of greenish-
brown resembling dying kelp shivered in the lee of
well-worn boulders, offering the only defiance to the
terribly-near sterility of naked space.

Sixteen eyes studied the unimpressive surroundings
until they were satisfied as to its harmlessness. McCoy
pointed to the east.

"There it is, Jim."

A low, rambling group of single-story interconnect-
ing building modules thrust out of the sand nearby.
They clustered near a huge metallic bubble like termites
around a bloated queen.

Kirk sniffed at the odd, unsatisfying atmosphere.
"Maybe I'm wrong," he muttered. "I hope so:" He
took a step toward the buildings.

Displaced air let out a soprano scream as a blue
beam passed near his right shoulder. It struck a boul-
der behind, sending rock splinters flying. One crewman
clutched at his shoulder as he spun to the sand.

"Take cover! Spread out and return fire!" Kirk
yelled, even as he dove for the nearest clump of rocks.
Spock was at his side, his phaser out and firing as

he hit the ground. McCoy had hold of the injured crewman's legs and was pulling him to shelter, analyzing the man's surface wound at the same time.

Kirk peered around the left side of a hunk of basalt. The source of the beams was the near bank of a dry streambed. Silhouettes of the beam-wielders were readily identifiable. Phaser beams began to strike the edge of the bank, fusing sand and gravel and sending rock fragments flying. The Klingon landing party was well protected.

"It would appear that your initial estimate of Commander Kumara was correct, Captain," Spock observed as his beam singed the hair of a too-anxious Klingon.

"Yes. Still, it's not like him to assume a formal defensive position like this and slug it out. More likely we surprised him just as his party set down. Spock, if this fight goes against him, I don't think he would hesitate to destroy the Delminnens to keep them and their device from falling into non-Imperial hands. I'm going to try to get them clear of that complex before the Klingons decide to blow it to bits. Give me all the covering fire you can."

There was a pause while the instructions were relayed to the other members of the landing party. Then they unleashed a furious burst of phaser firepower as Kirk dashed for the nearest wall of the modular cluster.

Something warm went by his right ear, humming like a wasp. He dove, rolled, and came up behind the wall of the outermost structure. A quick glance around the edge revealed that the Klingons were fully occupied with the rest of the *Enterprise*'s landing party.

Reaching up, Kirk felt his ear. A blister was beginning to form, so near had the beam been. But he still had all of him.

Sliding along the wall in an attempt to remain concealed from those inside as well as everyone outside, he finally reached a thick window. It took a moment to make the proper adjustment to his hand phaser. Then, using it like a torch, he carefully melted down the window plastic.

A cautious peek showed the interior of a comfortable, denlike room. It was dark and deserted. Resetting his phaser on stun, he put one leg over the sill and eased himself into the room. It was empty.

Kirk took out his communicator and flipped it open. Suddenly someone screamed.

Sound, left; door, closed; reaction—that which is quickest rather than that which is planned.

The door opened easily. At the far end of the half-laboratory, half-living quarters, Kumara was supporting an unconscious Van Delminnen while wrestling with a struggling woman. Her features were softer, less aquiline than Delminnen's, but the resemblance was unmistakable.

Kumara was juggling his communicator along with the two bodies. Looking up, he saw Kirk framed in the doorway and froze.

Thawing was rapid. "Up, fool," he shouted into his communicator. "Beam us up or it's your head! Beam—" He was forced to drop his communicator in order to hold on to Char Delminnen.

Kirk was running toward the trio as they began to fade. "Scotty—up!" was all he had time to yell into his own communicator.

On board the *Enterprise*, Scott heard the brief command and spoke to his assistant. "Don't stand there like you've seen Loch Nessie, mon—let's get him up!" Sure hands commenced rapid manipulation of precision controls.

The figure of Kirk began to scintillate at the edges. At the same time, he threw himself, arms outstretched toward the three figures. Confused energies interacted in a brilliant display of condensed high-power pyrotechnics.

The reaction on board the *Enterprise* was smaller but no less spectacular. Lights that should have remained dark flashed brightly on the transporter console. Gauges which ought to have stayed quiescent suddenly danced as if afflicted by a mechanical Saint Vitus' dance. Sparks arched indecently from switch to closed contact and back again.

Scott's mind was in turmoil, but he held himself steady as he adjusted, realigned, and compensated, glancing nervously from the console to the still-vacant transporter alcove.

"Come on, Captain," he whispered tightly, "come *on.*"

He shoved one switch forward another notch. Four jumbled, indistinct shapes began to form within the alcove. They flickered in and out like boat lights in a fog.

"Engineering," he called to the open directional pickup, "Main Transporter Room, Chief Scott speaking. I want all the power transporter circuits will carry—or you'll be carryin' it with your hands next time!"

He shoved the crucial control into the red. As he did so, the four shapes grew more distinct, almost materialized.

The control hit the far end of the slot.

Metal ran like water, and intricate components turned to blobs of expensive slag. Tiny popping sounds came from within the console's base.

Kirk and a young woman solidified. Simultaneously, the other two indistinct images abruptly disappeared. Kirk wavered, his leg muscles rippling uncontrollably; then he collapsed to the floor, rolling out of the alcove. The woman fell on top of him.

"Captain!" Waving at the acrid smoke which now curled about the ruined console, Scott staggered around its edge, moving to a wall intercom. "Sick Bay . . . corpsman to the Main Transporter Room, on the double! Chief Kyle?"

"Here, sir," came the reply.

"Stand by second-level transporter . . . we've still got a landing party on the surface."

"Standing by, sir."

Spock studied the ravine ahead, turned, and called back to the rest of the team. "Cease firing . . . they've transported clear." He turned his attention toward the cluster of structures as a figure wriggled up alongside him.

"You think they've given up the fight, Spock?" wondered McCoy, his attention likewise riveted on the buildings.

"The fight . . . yes," commented Spock unsurely. "The war . . . I don't know. I wish I knew as much about this Klingon Kumara as the captain seems to. He may already be back on board . . . someone used a communicator a little while ago."

A tremendous explosion caused both men to bury their heads in the sand. Bits of metal and plastic and other nonmetallic debris, mixed with sand and rock, rained down on them.

They looked up. When the dust and smoke cleared, they saw a small crater where the metal bubble and its attendant structures had stood.

McCoy looked questioningly at Spock. "If the captain's *not* already on board . . ."

Spock merely nodded, flipped open his communicator. "Spock to *Enterprise* . . . beam us up. What"—he stumbled over the words, an indication of how he felt—"what word on the captain?"

"He's aboard and all right, Mr. Spock," came the filtered burr of Chief Engineer Scott, much to the relief of both men. "But somethin' . . . I dinna know what yet . . . went wrong with the transporter. Nurse Chapel is treatin' him. Stand by to beam up."

They materialized in a room different from the one they had left. Disorientation lasted only a moment; then Spock addressed the security team. "Ensign Gemas, dismiss your people. You," he said to the injured crewman, "report to Sick Bay and have that shoulder treated."

"Tell whoever's on duty to use the extractor, son," McCoy added. "You've still got some stone shrapnel imbedded in the muscle." The man nodded, wincing painfully.

McCoy, was the first to enter the rubble of the still-smoke-filled Transporter Room, saw the two seated figures propped against the wall flanking the alcove.

"Jim!" He hurried over to the captain, knelt, and looked at Nurse Chapel.

"Nervous shock, Doctor," she explained in a professional tone, "complicated by extended trauma of unknown origin."

"Thank you, Chapel. I'll take over here. Help her." He indicated the blank-eyed woman slumped against the wall, and Chapel moved to do so. Spock bent to study the woman also.

McCoy examined Kirk hurriedly, pulled a hypo from kit Chapel had brought, and administered it. While he waited for the drug to take effect, he glanced curiously back toward the transporter console, where Scott and his assistant were busily examining its cauterized innards.

"What happened, Mr. Scott?"

The chief engineer stared a moment longer at the intricate circuit board—its fluid-state switches a mass of thin goo, its hundreds of microchips forming metal stalactites on its edge—and he shook his head dolefully.

"I dinna know, Doctor. One minute there were four figures beamin' in, then they'd fade almost to nothing, then grow solid again. In an' out, in an' out, no matter how fine we calibrated the resolution or how much power we poured into materialization. I finally decided to pull 'em in with everythin' we had. The captain came through all right and so did the young lady, but the other two, whoever they were, disappeared. Dinna ask me where to."

McCoy would have pressed for details, but Kirk was groaning and moving his head.

"Doctor," Spock declared with concern, "this one is not responding to stimuli." Chapel indicated agreement.

"Get a stretcher detail up here, Chapel, and have her moved to Sick Bay."

"Yes, Doctor." She moved to issue the necessary order. Spock leaned close to Kirk and looked up at McCoy.

"He's coming around. I don't know what happened to them when the transporter went crazy, but the effects were just this side of overpowering."

A pair of medical techs appeared with a wheelabout between them, and McCoy watched as the woman was gently placed on the mobile bed and rolled from the room.

Kirk let out a loud moan, diverting their attention.

"Captain, can you reason?" inquired Spock anxiously. "Do you know where you are?"

Kirk only groaned again.

Spock looked worriedly at McCoy. "What are the possible effects on someone held in transport for too long, Doctor?"

McCoy shrugged slightly. "No one knows for certain what happens to the mind in extended transport, Spock. Transporters used under normal conditions are foolproof. Under abnormal conditions, we just don't know enough about what actually takes place. There are two known cases of people who were in transport when there was an all-systems power failure, backups included. They were finally brought in, but in a coma from which they never emerged."

He looked back to Kirk, just as the captain opened his eyes and blinked. "Where are the others?"

At the sound of Kirk's voice, Scott left analysis of the ruined transporter console to his assistant. "Thank the saints you're all right, Captain."

"Thank *you*, Scotty." Kirk stood up, rubbing at his forehead. "You've heard of locking someone in a water-filled, lightless tank so that they experience near-total sensory deprivation, Bones?"

"I'm familiar with the therapy, Jim."

"Well, I just experienced the opposite extreme." He looked around the room. "Am I the only one who came through?"

"No, Captain," Scott informed him. "There was a young lady as well. And there appeared to be at least two other figures, but for some reason the transporter malfunctioned and we couldn't hold them." He looked at the deck. "I fear they've gone to where no one can find them."

"No, Scotty, and don't blame yourself. Your transporter didn't fail. Our friend Kumara was all set to have himself and the Delminnens beamed back to his ship while we supposedly sat around and waited for the big reunion. I inconveniently barged in on him as he was preparing to do just that.

"As soon as he saw me he ordered his techs to beam himself and the Delminnens up. I didn't have time to do anything but make the same request of you, Scotty, and take a dive for the three of them, hoping our transporter could overpower theirs. Looks like it ended up a tie." He glanced over at Spock. "I see you got back safely Spock. Casualties?"

"One injured, Captain," the first officer reported. "Not seriously."

"Good. Maintain red alert. Where's the girl . . . Char Delminnen?"

"In Sick Bay by now, Jim," McCoy explained. "She's suffering from shock also. I ran a quick test on her, and I suppose your shock was induced by the same thing. Some of your blood got switched around in all the transporting confusion—veins to arteries and vice versa. Your shock was induced by temporary oxygen starvation." He shook his head. "Wait till they read about that in the *Starfleet Medical Journal*."

"Will she be all right?"

"I expect so. She's probably coming out of it even as we're talking."

"Captain . . . ?" Scott looked pensive.

"Yes, what is it, Scotty?"

"You'll pardon me for sayin' so, but you took the devil of a chance intersectin' transporter fields like that. No wonder everythin' went overload. You could've had a lot more than your hemoglobin switched around."

"I know, Scotty," Kirk replied solemnly. "I knew it at the time. But there was nothing else to do. At least Char Delminnen's safe."

"Wonderful for her," McCoy noted bitterly, "but the one we came for is either dead or, more likely, on board the Klingon cruiser."

"A situation we're going to have to rectify, Bones."

"Message from the bridge, sir," came a call from an

ensign standing by the wall intercom. Kirk hurried to take his position.

"Transporter Room, Kirk here."

Sulu's voice was excited, tense. "Captain, the Klingon cruiser appears to be picking up speed. Indications are she's retracing her original approach."

"Lay in a tracking course, Mr. Sulu. Don't let her slow speed fool you—Kumara's trying to get into the shadow of the gas giant. If he can do that, he'll move to maximum speed immediately, before we can get a fix on him. Don't let him out of detector range."

"Yes, *sir!*"

Kirk moved to rejoin McCoy and Spock.

"What is it, Jim?"

"Van Delminnen's on board the Klingon ship all right. Kumara's now trying to sneak out of the system and run for cover. We're going after him, Bones."

"Was that indicated in the orders, Captain?" wondered Spock.

Kirk threw his first officer a hard look. "The orders were to bring back the Delminnens, Mr. Spock, utilizing whatever methods were necessary."

"A blanket authorization with regard to the persons of the Delminnens, Captain," Spock persisted, "but does that justify pursuit of an enemy ship?"

"They can quibble over the semantics later, Mr. Spock," Kirk declared. "*After* Van Delminnen is safely delivered to the nearest Starfleet base." He stalked toward the lift.

A sudden surge rocked them as the lift opened onto the bridge. Kirk moved immediately to his command position while Spock took his place at the science station. McCoy hovered nearby, feeling helpless as usual, despite the benefits his presence always brought to a tense bridge.

"Report, Mr. Sulu."

"Captain, as soon as we started to move, they increased their speed slightly. I adjusted our own to match, at which point they accelerated again. Thanks to your warning, Mr. Arex and I anticipated it and matched velocity once more. We are still within detector range, traveling at warp-six." He checked a readout. "But we are not making up any distance on them."

"I didn't expect we would be, Mr. Sulu," replied Kirk. "They're certain to be traveling at their maximum safe speed . . . for now. That's going to have to change. Mr. Spock?"

"Yes, Captain?"

"Did you discover anything in the Delminnen complex which might have been the weapon?"

"Unfortunately, we never had the opportunity to look. Do not look alarmed, Captain—neither did the Klingons."

Kirk relaxed visibly.

"The Delminnen residence, laboratories, and any conceivable weapon were completely destroyed by a timed device planted by the Klingons soon after you entered the outer structure. We were unable to prevent the destruction. Considering the manner in which the Klingons departed, it seems reasonable to assume that the device was intended to detonate with all of us inside the complex. It seems rather wasteful. I am surprised the Klingons did not attempt to recover the device itself."

"I'm not, Spock. Kumara never liked to take chances. Having captured one major piece, he opted to blow up the board. Obviously, he's convinced Delminnen can be persuaded to give him the plans for the device." He stared grimly at the starfield displayed on the main screen. "The Klingons can be most persuasive."

He paused, mulling multiples of light over in his mind. "Spock, what is the nearest Klingon military base of importance in this region?"

"A moment, Captain." Spock bent over the library computer and reported quickly. "According to what information we have, there is a naval base of considerable size on Shahkur Nine."

"Do we have coordinates for said world?"

"Yes, Captain. They are imprecise, however."

"*Hmm.*" Kirk turned to the helm. "Mr. Arex, assuming Shahkur lies at the closest possible point given by those imprecise stats, compute the time we can expect to have before ships from that world could be expected to rendezvous with Kumara—and with the *Enterprise*."

Arex's triple hands worked busily at the navigation console, extrapolating from a simple yet crucial series of numbers. He expressed no worry, no excitement over the results. That was the Edoan way. Emotions were subdued, but not supressed as they were among the inhabitants of Vulcan.

"Assuming both vessels maintain their current velocity, Captain, I give us no more than forty-eight standard hours."

"Maximum?"

"Given the restrictions of questionable coordinates for Shahkur . . . yes. That figure is for vessels of the *Enterprise*'s class out from Shahkur. Lesser classes would take longer, of course."

"But we can't assume they'll send lesser-class ships." He glanced back at Spock. "This Shahkur Nine is supposed to be a *major* base, Mr. Spock?"

"Yes, Captain."

Kirk looked resigned. "Then we'd better assume Kumara will meet additional cruisers in a couple of days. That gives us very little time to rescue Delminnen."

"Or to kill him, Captain," reminded Spock quietly.

Kirk's voice was flat. "Or to kill him."

It was silent on the bridge for several of those forty-eight hours. Silent, but far from inactive, as Kirk and Spock considered the options open to them in the shrinking time available.

The stillness was too much for McCoy, finally. He had checked half a dozen times on the condition of the injured security specialist and paid an equal number of visits to Char·Delminnen—all a waste of time, as the specialist's injury was minor and Nurse Chapel had the woman under mild sedation.

"Well, what are we going to do, Jim? We could call

for help ourselves, but that would bring a Federation
fleet into contact with a Klingon force of possibly equal
size. Then we'd have a nice little interstellar war on
our hands."

"I know, Bones. That's why we're going to have to
resolve this one alone, without help."

"If we run into three or four Klingon cruisers, it'll
be resolved all right," McCoy observed sardonically.

"Captain," Spock began, "if I may suggest the obvious . . . ?"

Both men turned to look at him.

"If we go to emergency power, we should be able to
get within phaser range."

"All we need for that to work, Spock, is to have a
normal, belligerent, cocky commander on board the
Klingon ship. Instead, we have to contend with
Kumara. I tell you, Spock, we can't apply the usual
standards here!

"If we go to emergency power, you know what will
happen? Kumara will laugh fit to split his collar. He
would love to see us burn out our nacelles trying to get
within phaser range. The moment we got close enough
to tickle his tail, *he'd* go on emergency power and keep
right on running until overload. Then we'd both drift
along on impulse power with charred converters—
straight toward Shahkur Nine and the oncoming Klingon relief force.

"As much faith as I have in Scotty and his engineers, I can't risk that." Kirk's brow furrowed. "But
Bones is right. We can't continue on like this without
trying something. Let me know, Mr. Spock, how this
sounds to you . . ."

VI

There was quiet jubilation on the bridge of the Klingon cruiser. Everyone on board knew that the mission
had been partly successful. And if the presence of the
peculiar human on board wasn't proof enough, the
presence of the trailing Federation cruiser was.

A certain amount of grumbling among the elder
officers followed the commander's refusal to turn and
engage their pursuer. Running away was alien to the
soul of any Klingon warrior. But the younger officers
harbored no such feelings, though they were as brave
as their superiors. They realized that Commander
Kumara's orders were best for the Empire, best for the
ship and best for themselves.

So they contented themselves with the knowledge
that their pursuer was traveling under the impetus of
mounting frustration.

"Commander," the helmsman reported smartly, "the
Federation ship is remaining constant relative to our
position. Should we utilize emergency power to increase the distance between us?"

"I'm rather fond of our present distance, Lieutenant
Kritt, and see no reason to change it. We will maintain
our present speed unless we are *compelled* to do otherwise, and we will maintain it without straining our
resources. Restrain from public exhibition of your
foolishness, and think."

"I abase myself, Honored Commander," the helmsman replied as he strove to comprehend Kumara's
point.

For his part, the commander continued his idle study
of the viewscreen. His rear scanners showed the pursuing *Enterprise,* only a distant, barely moving dot
against the blackness of space—space which one day

would be a part of the Empire, as the Great Gods intended it should be.

"Lieutenant, there is a game humans play, a game Vulcans play. It is called chess. Ever hear of it?"

Kritt turned from his console, confident that the heathen Federation ship was still a safe distance behind, and succeeded in looking earnestly puzzled.

"A human game? Hardly, Commander. Why do you ask?"

"I suspected you had not. Few of us have, preferring to languish in contempt of anything not Klingon; and that is much to be deplored. You might look it up in the archives sometime. The knowledge would do you good.

"Were Captain Kirk and I presently to be engaged in such a game, I would say I have him dangerously in check, with the next move being his."

"Ah," observed Kritt, brightening, "it is something like *bagap*, then?"

Kumara considered, then indicated approval. "There are similarities, yes, though *bagap* is a much faster game. And chess is played with little wooden idols on a plastic or celluloid field, instead of with live slaves."

"It sounds very dull."

"Be assured, it is not." Kumara's manner shifted abruptly from one of casual camaraderie and introspection to that of the complete dictator. "Under no circumstances are we to engage emergency power unless the *Enterprise* does so first! Make certain all concerned understand this implicitly!"

"At once, Commander," Kritt shot back, relaxing now that his superior was once more the model of Klingon leadership . . .

"Kumara," Kirk explained to the attentive Spock as McCoy listened in, "is difficult to surprise, but there's no reason to suppose that his subordinates are anything other than the usual Klingon ratings. That means they'll be contemptuous, secure in their present tactical position—and overconfident. I'm hoping that will also make them just lazy enough."

"Lazy enough for what, Jim?" McCoy wondered.

"You'll see. Mr. Spock, have the shuttlecraft readied for departure."

Spock's eyebrows lifted in surprise. "The *shuttlecraft*, Captain?"

"That's right. Make certain it's fully fueled."

Spock moved to his library-science station and directed his words to the intercom pickup. "First Officer Spock to Shuttle Bay. Prepare Shuttle One for immediate flight." He looked back across at Kirk.

"Pilot and course, Captain?"

"There will be no pilot, Spock. The shuttle will run on automatics which will be guided by the *Enterprise*'s battle computer."

"Now I'm thoroughly confused, Jim," McCoy muttered.

"With luck, the Klingons will be too, Bones. Mr. Arex, set a course for the shuttle: zero degrees inclination to plane of present course." Then he recited a plot which even McCoy was able to recognize.

"But . . . that's *our* present course, Jim."

Kirk smiled back at him. "I'm not fooling anyone, you see. The simplest device is often the best. Everyone keeps an eye out for the least obvious." He addressed the chair pickup. "Engineering?"

"Engineering, Scott here. Are we goin' to make a run at them finally, Captain?"

"After a fashion, Scotty. I'm going to want every milligram of push you can coax out of those engines in a few minutes. We're going to have to push them right to the limit."

"You'll have whatever you need, Captain."

At the rear of the *Enterprise*, twin clamshell doors slid back to reveal a high, well-lit chamber—the shuttlecraft hangar. Tiny wisps of frozen air, missed by the recyclers, puffed out from the crack which appeared between the doors.

Spock listened for a moment, then turned to report, "Shuttlecraft One ready for launch, Captain."

Kirk took a deep, hopeful breath. "All right. Ready, everyone. Mr. Sulu, I want full emergency power."

"Aye, sir." Sulu activated the necessary controls. A steady, rarely heard whine began to build on the bridge as the *Enterprise*'s immense engines labored to comply.

On board the Klingon cruiser, Lieutenant Kritt suddenly bent close over his console and stared intently at the readouts from the rear-facing scanners.

"Commander, the Federation ship is closing on us!" He paused to check the information with the helmsman. "Reports confirmed—they are increasing speed rapidly."

Kumara frowned slightly, and peered at the growing dot on the viewscreen. He searched his mind for possibilities, but found nothing but groundless conjecture.

"I had expected something more elaborate from James Kirk. Even so, he *is* pressed for time. He must know we will contact Shahkur Base and request reinforcement soon." He barked an order at Kritt. "Prepare to go on emergency power."

Sulu was busy studying the information his own scanners were sending back to him. "We're gaining on them, sir."

"Speed, Mr. Sulu?"

"Warp-seven ... coming up on warp-eight, maximum speed."

"Push her as far as she'll stand, Lieutenant."

Sulu shoved down the final switch, pressed the last button, and turned his attention to a bank of small dials. All were creeping steadily into the red at the end of each scale.

"Definitely closing on the Klingon ship, Captain," Arex reported with a touch of excitement.

"Engine temperature rising rapidly, Captain," Spock reported.

On board the Klingon cruiser, Kumara examined the flow of information and muttered into a pickup. "Stand by, Engineering. Not yet, Kritt," he added, noticing one of the navigator's hands hovering tensely over a control. "Learn patience and attain permanence."

"Converter temperature is nearing the melting point, Captain," Spock reported, not looking up from his instrumentation. "Coming up on phaser range. Shall I prepare to fire?"

"Negative, Mr. Spock." There was a beep at his arm. "What is it, Scotty?"

The chief engineer's worried voice sounded distantly over the speaker, distorted by the now deafening whine of the engines.

"Captain, we canna keep this up much longer without melting something critical!"

"Hold steady a bit longer, Scotty."

"A bit is all it'll be, Captain. Engineerin' out."

"Exalted Commander," a worried Kritt said, looking anxiously from his console back at Kumara, "they'll be within phaser range any minute."

"Gently, Lieutenant, gently."

Spock's tone never changed, only the information was modulated. "Engine temperature nearing the critical point, Captain." He turned and looked at Kirk, with an expression that said more lucidly than words, Do now whatever you've got a mind to do.

Kirk hesitated no longer.

"Launch shuttlecraft!"

Spock gave the order and reported promptly, "Shuttlecraft away and locked on course."

"Cut emergency power ... reduce speed to warp-six."

"Reducing speed," Sulu responded.

"Engine temperature dropping rapidly, Captain," Spock announced. As he did so, the temperature on the bridge also seemed to drop noticeably.

"Engineering, report," Kirk said into the pickup. There was a long moment before Scott's tired voice replied.

"Engineerin' ... We almost lost one of the dilithium chambers. You cut it mighty near, Captain."

"Sorry, Scotty. Had to. Congratulate everyone back there for me. For all of us."

"I will, Captain . . . as soon as they stop tremblin'. Engineering out." Scott clicked off, moved to the central console, and planted a wet kiss of gratitude on a certain gauge which had yet again moved him one minute nearer a comfortable retirement.

"What now, Jim?" McCoy wondered aloud, staring at the viewscreen. Their quarry was no longer a distant glowing pinpoint, but now a definite inimical silhouette.

"I'd estimate about five minutes, Bones." Kirk chewed his lower lip and tried to see deeper than the ship's scanners . . .

On board the Klingon cruiser, Lieutenant Kritt leaned back in his stiff, unyielding seat and spoke with satisfaction. "Commander, the Federation ship's position is once again constant with respect to ours. They are no longer closing distance."

If he expected his exalted superior to look pleased, he was disappointed. Sometimes Kumara could be as impassive as a Vulcan. The commander gave every sign of having expected the good news.

"I thought they couldn't maintain that speed much longer, Lieutenant," he commented easily, before turning his attention to the intercom. "Engineering, stand down. Emergency power will not be required." He looked back at the screen, murmuring half to himself, "Nice bluff, James Kirk, but you should know better than to try to panic me."

"Pardons, Commander," Kritt wondered, "but aren't we going to utilize emergency power to reopen the distance between our ships? They are extremely close now."

"Extremely, but not dangerously so, Lieutenant. Have you learned nothing? They could only have hoped to prod us into straining our own resources—something," he added smugly, "we will not do. So long as we remain out of phaser range, they might as well be a dozen system-units behind, for all the harm they can do us. Nor do I believe their vessel has the capacity to repeat that maneuver again before we are con-

tacted by relief ships from Shahkur Base." He looked
well pleased with himself.

"Then there is the delicious irony of the situation."

Kritt looked confused. "Irony, Commander?"

"Do you not see it? Fah! I am assisted by blind men.
Not only has their attempt to pressure us failed
completely, Lieutenant, but now they must bear the
additional torment of following us at much closer
range. Close enough for their scanners to read our reg-
istration numbers—close enough for them to sense our
smiles, you see."

Kritt turned back to his readouts and studied them,
his gaze shifting thoughtfully from the tiny unemotional
figures back to the main screen with its portrait of the
pursuing *Enterprise*. "I think I do, Commander. I think
. . ."

Spock noted the latest readings of separation and reported, "The enemy vessel is maintaining course and
speed, Captain."

"No evidence of increasing her speed?"

"No, Captain. Apparently they are content to remain at this distance."

"Good. Mr. Spock, prepare for remote converter
override of the shuttlecraft's engine. Remove safeties
and cancel fail-safes. Mr. Sulu, *now* you can energize
the forward phasers."

Realization dawned on the helmsman's face, and he
bent to the task gleefully. The purpose was slower in
coming to McCoy; Spock had already guessed it.

"An excellent idea, Captain," the first officer commented approvingly. "It requires only that the Klingons
act as Klingons. Given that, the possibilities for success
are substantial."

"So *that's* it!" McCoy declared. "You really think it
will change the status quo, Jim?"

"I'm hopeful, Bones. A lot depends on their instrumentation being so tied up with monitoring our every
sneeze that they'll overlook an object the size of the
shuttle. They know we're well out of photon-torpedo

range—but the shuttle's engine is capable of covering a good deal more space.

"Of course, it would be a useless effort if Kumara's ship was undertaking defensive maneuvers. But it's not. They're simply cruising along an unwavering course."

"Shuttle closing on enemy vessel, sir," Arex reported.

Everyone on the bridge stared at the screen, trying to spot the minute spark that would be the shuttle. Detectors tracked it easily, though, where the naked eye failed.

At one end of the *Klathas*'s bridge an officer suddenly squinted, staring hard and uncertainly at an unexpectedly active screen, noting a small but potentially significant reading. It might be nothing. Probably was, in which case he risked exposing himself to embarrassment and ridicule.

On the other hand, if the instrumentation was doing its job . . . and mechanicals were immune to insult.

"Commander?" he finally said, electing to tempt the gods.

"Yes? What is it, Korreg?"

"Exalted One, I wish you would give your opinion of this. It appears to be a very oddly formed meteoric body which—"

Kumara barely had time to look startled before dashing down to stare over the scanner-control officer's shoulder. When he saw the activated screen and matched it against the reading nearby, he turned a light purple.

"IDIOT!"

Korreg winced, not sure whether he'd exercised the proper option.

Kumara didn't have time to enlighten him. That would come soon enough . . . perhaps lethally.

"Engineering!" he roared into the intercom. "Full emergency power—maximum thrust!"

"But, Commander," a hesitant voice replied, "you just said—"

"I want full emergency thrust immediately or I'll personally pull your eyes from your head, Kanndad!"

"Ye—yes, Commander! At once!"

"Captain," Sulu cried, "the Klingon ship is increasing her speed. They appear to be going on emerg—"

"Present shuttlecraft position, Lieutenant!" Kirk barked, cutting the helmsman off.

"Shuttle is nearing critical radius, Captain," Sulu reported, more in control of himself now, though the tenseness remained in his voice. "Wait . . . distance is increasing. Klingon cruiser beginning to pull—"

"Spock! Exercise engine override—*now!*"

The first officer touched a switch. Kilometers of circuitry sent a single, brief signal to the racing shuttle, still traveling ahead of the now slowed *Enterprise* at her launch speed of warp-eight. The on-board shuttlecraft computer was simple compared to the massive machine mind on board the starship, but it was fully capable of interpreting that concise command.

A few relays opened, protesting controls were ignored, normal modifiers were shunted aside as the shuttle obediently self-destructed. As it did so, a stunning flash of white radiance momentarily blinded the *Enterprise*'s forward scanners.

The effects of that silent explosion on the *Klathas* were somewhat more extreme.

"Report, Mr. Sulu," Kirk demanded, mentally crossing his fingers. "Status of Klingon cruiser?"

The helmsman double-checked his instrumentation to be certain before announcing, "She's losing speed, Captain . . . dropping below warp-seven . . . below warp-six. We're moving into phaser range."

"It worked, Jim," McCoy observed, a note of satisfaction and admiration in his voice.

Kirk didn't sound enthusiastic. "We don't know how well it worked, Bones. The range was extreme, and expanding even as I gave Spock the order. We've obviously disabled her, damaged her engines, but her offensive weaponry may still be intact and fully operational. Now comes the difficult part."

"You mean attacking?"

"No. Trying to convince Kumara that he's got to

surrender. Stand by forward phasers and torpedo banks. Mr. Sulu."

"Standing by, sir," replied the helmsman firmly.

Emergency ventilators were rapidly clearing the *Klathas*'s bridge of smoke and dangerous freed gases. The sounds of coughing and the crew's gasps for decent air provided an unnerving accompaniment to Kumara's efforts to regain the command seat. He had been ungently thrown from that position when the shuttlecraft's engine exploded.

Painfully, he hauled himself to a sitting position in the chair, favoring the arm he had fallen on. A careful yet rapid survey showed that the bridge was still operational and casualties were minor.

What it was like at the rear of the *Klathas*, the place that had borne the brunt of the concussion caused by superheated gases and vaporized solids, he could well imagine.

"Speed . . . speed is still falling, Commander," a battered Kritt reported slowly, feeling his bruised jaw with one hand. Kumara activated the intercom and was gratified to find that it worked perfectly.

"Engineering, damage report." Silence shouted back at him from the stern of the ship. He tried again. "Engineering, this is your commander. Kanndad, what's the difficulty back there? I need this ship back up to speed in ten *aines* or I'll have you all fed to the converters!"

A worn, rasping voice finally replied. It was tinged with a vaguely insubordinate sarcasm. "Kanndad here Captain. We've sustained major damage to both engine nacelles. This ship won't make good cruising speed for several hundred *aines*, *if* the damage is repairable at all, and *if* most of my key personnel haven't been too seriously injured. What happened?"

"Never mind that now," Kumara told him irritably. He did not take note of his engineer's sarcastic response. He didn't have time for such luxuries. "Other than the drive, what is our power status?"

Kanndad turned silent again, apparently consulting someone out of pickup range.

"Eighty percent, Commander," he finally reported. Kumara took some comfort from that announcement. They were crippled but still armed.

Kritt spoke into the nearly clear atmosphere. "Federation ship closing to battle range, Commander." A pause; then, "They are transmitting."

Kumara could guess the nature of that transmission. Well, if Kirk thought the *Klathas* was drifting helplessly, he had an unpleasant surprise in store.

"I can see that she's closing, offspring of a worm's slave. As to the transmission, we'll answer it all right. Arm all rearward projectors and fire at will. And, Korreg, for once in your misbegotten life, see if you can hit something smaller than a blue star. Full power to the defensive screens." He stared at the viewscreen, which now clearly showed the ominous form of the approaching *Enterprise*.

"It is just," he muttered, too softly for anyone to hear, "that a ship of fools be commanded by a fool."

But if they survived the coming fight, he vowed, Kirk would not fool him again . . .

VII

Sulu carefully noted the sliding dial which indicated battle position relative to their quarry. "Inside range, Captain."

Kirk hesitated. He had no idea how badly the *Klathas* was damaged or how many serious injuries her crew had already suffered. "Uhura, any response to our transmission?"

"Not yet, Captain. Possibly their own communications have been damaged."

"Possibly. Or Kumara could be—"

A dull *crump* sounded, and the bridge was rocked by a wave of energy. Lights flickered momentarily before steadying.

"We've absorbed a full attack from the Klingons' rear projector banks, Captain," Spock informed them. "Our screens are holding tight."

"Returning fire, Captain," said Sulu, adjusting massive instruments of destruction with delicate fingers.

Kirk half smiled. "That's our answer. I should have known Kumara would choose to open negotiations in his own way. What's their speed, Lieutenant?"

Sulu checked a different set of readouts. "Holding at about warp-five, Captain."

"We have to reduce their speed still further," Kirk instructed everyone. "Otherwise, we'll simply fight a running battle until the ships from Shahkur meet up with Kumara. We have to weaken him significantly, weaken him to the point where he'll have no choice but to surrender. We have slightly more mobility, Mr. Sulu. Use it."

"Doing my best, sir," the thoroughly occupied helmsman responded. "We'll cut them down."

That section of space was filled for the next hour with a hellish display of barely controlled energies,

99

beams of blue and red piercingly brilliant through the stark blackness. Occasional eruptions of lambent cloud appeared on the exterior of each vessel whenever offensive probing beams contacted the argumentative energies of a defensive screen.

Sulu used the *Enterprise*'s superior speed carefully, teaming with the ship's battle computer to confuse the Klingons' retaliatory efforts while optimizing the *Enterprise*'s own attacks. There was little the Klingons could do to compensate. If they lowered their speed to throw off the *Enterprise*'s attacks, they conceded even more mobility to the Federation ship, gave her battle computer another chip to play ... and, most important, lengthened the time between themselves and the Shahkur rendezvous.

At 62.24 minutes into the running battle, a phaser beam partially penetrated a severely strained defensive screen to strike one of the *Klatha*'s engine nacelles a glancing blow. That glancing blow killed twenty technicians and wounded as many others. The local damage was extreme.

Kumara knew they had taken a considerable hit from the wrench it communicated to the bridge. This time he managed to hold his position.

"Kanndad . . . Kanndad!" he yelled into the intercom. It gave back only a threatening crackle.

"Communications to that part of the ship temporarily out," Kritt reported. "Working to reestablish. Secondary engineering reports left converter potential critically damaged by phaser fire. We're going to lose more than half our remaining speed. Engineering reports that unless total engine shutdown occurs within five *du-aines,* to permit repairs, all light-multiple drive capability will be lost."

"When primary engineering communications are reestablished, instruct Engineer Kanndad to do his utmost, Lieutenant."

"Yes, sir," a disgruntled Kritt acknowledged. "Maintaining fire. Shifting to compensate for weakened screen."

Kumara heard the words, looked at the faces of his immediate subordinates, and knew that unless they effected a drastic reversal of the present battle conditions, he would be forced to surrender or ship-suicide.

Undoubtedly, Kirk would be prepared for any new tricks. Very well, then . . . he would try an old one.

"Attention, all stations."

Harried, dispirited faces turned to look at him as he activated general intership intercom, sending his voice throughout the battle-weary vessel.

"Attention. Burial details and all nonoffensive-action personnel. You will begin a complete canvass of the ship and gather all nonessential items—repeat, gather all nonessential items. Strip your cabins, the corridors, storage chambers of anything and everything not integral to live support or ship operations." His voice darkened.

"I am being generous in not including certain personnel in this classification. However, if this order is not efficiently complied with, that may change.

"All items are to be collected and transferred to the Auxiliary Landing Craft Hangar. Life Support Station: You will prepare to vent surplus atmosphere through surface vents in conjunction with the ejection of surplus material via the landing-craft hanger." He checked his wrist chronometer, reading it through the scratches which now covered its face.

"Ejection of material and atmosphere is to take place in . . . three-quarters *du-aines*. It will include any personnel remaining in the lock, so I strongly suggest you move rapidly. Your commander and officers salute you, warriors of Klingon!"

He switched off and turned, to see the bridge complement hard at their stations, continuing the fight. All but Kritt, who was eyeing him expectantly.

"We cannot outrun them any more, Lieutenant," Kumara explained, "nor does it appear we will be able to make contact with the relief force in time. Therefore, everything on this vessel except the crew is going to commit suicide. My own private stock of Gellian *vitz* included."

Kritt almost asked, "To what end," then decided that it would become evident. The predatory gleam in the commander's eyes, however, was more encouraging than any words could have been.

The time arrived. "Auxiliary Landing Craft Hangar reporting," came a voice from one of the bridge speakers. "Ejection of material accomplished."

"Surplus atmosphere discharged," came the word from Life Support Control.

"Now," Kumara said to the general intercom, "all power to everything but minimal life-support systems is to be shut down."

"But, Commander," Korreg protested as the lights on the bridge began to dim, "what about our projectors, our defenses?"

"I said *everything*, Lieutenant." He turned his gaze to the main screen. "I only hope they don't decide to take the easy way out. I am depending on Captain Kirk to act like a human . . ."

Spock's eyebrows twitched once as the new information appeared on his readouts. "Captain, detectors indicate that the Klingons are losing their internal power. Defensive screens fading."

"I'll say," said an exuberant Sulu. "That last burst went right through her starboard-crew section."

"Cease fire, Mr. Sulu!" Kirk ordered quickly. "I'll not fire on a helpless ship . . . not even a Klingon's."

"It could be a trick, Jim," McCoy commented cautiously.

"Yes, it could, Bones." Kirk studied the small image of the *Klathas* thoughtfully. "But you heard what Sulu just said . . . apparently, we can penetrate her weakened screens at will. Though I wonder if—"

"Sir!" There was an undercurrent of excitement in the helmsman's voice. "Detectors indicate the *Klathas* is trailing a large amount of metallic and plastic debris."

"Confirmed, Captain," Spock announced. "I have also noted a steady stream of frozen atmosphere leaking from several locations on the cruiser's exterior."

Elation reigned on the bridge, mingled with exclamations of satisfaction. Only Kirk—and Spock, naturally—betrayed no sign of pleasure.

"Well, what are we hesitating for, Jim?" McCoy finally asked. "They're in no condition to argue surrender terms."

Kirk shook his head slowly. "I don't like it, Bones. It's too sudden, too easy. One minute they're fighting with everything they have, and the next, without being struck a severe blow, they seem to be coming apart."

"We can't tell how much running damage they've suffered, Jim."

"Maybe not, Bones." He made a decision. "Lieutenant Uhura, try to raise the Klingon bridge." Uhura moved to comply. She looked back and shrugged slightly several moments later.

"Negative, Captain. Their communications are dead. I can't find evidence of any activity, not even on-board closed transmissions, not a hand communicator . . . nothing. That ship's as mute as a coffin."

Which it could very well be by now, Kirk mused. But to be *certain* . . . how to be certain . . .

"The *Klathas* is losing speed rapidly, Captain," Arex indicated. "Dropping below warp-five . . . warp-four . . . continuing to lose speed, sir."

"Stop looking so glum, Jim," McCoy said. "They're the ones experiencing all the trouble, not us."

"It certainly looks that way, Bones." He sighed. "All right. Take us in close, Mr. Sulu. Keep your phasers trained on her bridge and bring us in just outside of transporter range."

The *Enterprise* promptly cut her own speed to match that of the rapidly slowing *Klathas*. The eyes studying this gradual shift were equally intent on both sides, but the glint of eagerness lay in those on board the Klingon cruiser.

"That's right, Captain Kirk," Kumara was murmuring softly, watching as the dim screen showed the *Enterprise* edging cautiously nearer, "come close . . . a bit more, that's right. No need to hurry. We'll have our reunion yet . . . minus the *vitz*, I fear."

Spock abruptly did something that he did only on rare occasions: He raised his voice. "Captain, preliminary analysis of the debris from the Klingon ship."

"Go ahead, Mr. Spock."

The first officer paused to recheck his information. It was nonspecific, general, but, for all that, of dangerous significance. "Sensors indicate that the detritus consists of personal possessions, supplies, spare fabricating material, and assorted other non-vital equipment."

"So?" an uncomprehending McCoy blurted.

"Not only is there nothing of vital concern to ship operations present, Doctor, but the drifting material appears to be wholly intact and undamaged."

Fact and reason formed critical mass in Kirk's whirling mind. "Mr. Sulu, initiate full evasive maneuvers, and fire at—"

Sulu's hand never reached the helm controls. Something loud and unyielding threw him sideways, slamming him into Arex's station. The Edoan navigator, thanks to triple limbs, managed to remain in his seat. Few of his companions succeeded in doing likewise.

Further explosions rocked the bridge, sending unsecured reports flying and tumbling the crew about like quicksilver on glass.

Quite without warning, the awesome barrage ceased.

Slowly, positions were regained. Reports began to come in from various stations around the bridge. They were not encouraging. The bridge illumination had dimmed considerably.

Other concerns were uppermost in Kirk's mind, however. "Mr. Sulu, Mr. Spock, report on disposition of enemy vessel."

Sulu had to compensate for several no longer usable instruments. Eventually he reported, "They have continued to drop speed, Captain. Apparently they are moving to operate on impulse power alone. Indications are that near-normal internal power has returned."

"Odd. Comments, Mr. Spock?"

"Sensors indicate that they have failed to reestablish other than minimal defensive screens, Captain. No sign of projector activity. This would seem to indicate that they have sustained major engine damage and have been compelled to shut down their drive to effect repairs. Our own speed is, however, dropping even more rapidly than theirs."

"At least they're not leaving us," Kirk muttered. "That's something, anyway. I concur with your assessment of the damage they must have suffered, Spock. Otherwise we wouldn't be here talking about it now. Kumara must have exhausted his power reserves with that last attack."

"Excuse me, sir," Uhura broke in. "Damage reports are beginning to come in from all levels. Decks Four through Seven indicate extensive though minor instrumentation damage. Firecontrol reports heavy damage to all phaser banks and photon-torpedo banks. Rear phasers are marginally operative, but the firecontrol computer has sustained major damage. Dr. McCoy reports . . ."

Kirk looked around at that. He hadn't even seen Bones leave the bridge.

". . . numerous minor injuries, mostly abrasive and concussive in nature. Several serious cases. He reports that he's preparing to supervise surgery."

"What about your own station, Lieutenant?"

Uhura checked her telltales and finally declared, "All deep-space Starfleet frequencies are inoperative due to broadcast-antenna damage combined with power loss. Local and on-board communications systems functional . . . if we don't get hit like that again."

"I don't expect we will, Lieutenant," he told her tightly, blinking as full illumination was restored to the bridge. He turned to study the battered shape of the *Klathas*. It seemed as though he could detect laughter drifting across the intervening space, floating right through the screen. That was impossible, of course. He told himself that as he waited for the most important report of all, the one which would determine their subsequent actions and options . . . if indeed they had any of the latter remaining.

The laughter refused to go away.

Even the beep of the chair intercom was a relief,

though he knew he couldn't expect any good news. He was right.

"That you, Scotty?"

"Aye, Captain." The chief engineer was standing at an auxiliary intercom station, watching busy specialists wrestling with battered components. His own previously sterile suit was laden with grime and colored liquid from fluid-state switches that now conducted only his disgust.

"D'ye want it all at once, or in installments?"

"Let's have the worst of it, Scotty." Kirk readied himself.

"That last projector hit was the worst, sir. Played hell with and damaged—never mind the details. I'll have a list of damaged components and material—and personnel—transferred forward soon as I get the chance.

"Simply put, we've got no warp-drive capability. Impulse power, yes, but we canna go nowhere verra fast for sometime. That's a minimum estimate. I hope you haven't got any pressin' engagements, Captain."

In spite of the grim report, Kirk managed a smile. "I'll send my regrets where necessary, Scotty. Do the best you can. If it's any consolation, the Klingons are apparently as badly damaged as we are. They're not going anywhere either. How's ship power?"

"Adequate for anythin' you want to try, Captain," the chief engineer declared reassuringly. "I heard about what happened up in Firecontrol. Too bad. The rear phasers'd work, if we had anythin' to work 'em with. Cut up the Klingons like veal on a butcher's block."

"We're not going to cut even that with those phasers for a good while, Scotty," Kirk reminded him. "Right now I'll settle for some mobility."

"Give it to you as soon as we can, Captain."

"I know you will, Scotty. Bridge out." Kirk searched his thoughts for a course of action, aware of the concerned glances the bridge personnel surreptitiously threw him . . . and found nothing.

"Summary and suggestions, Mr. Spock?"

The first officer replied smoothly, as though the consequences of near annihilation were an everyday event. "Engines dead, phasers inoperable, life-support systems sufficient. We can't run, we can't fight, but we are going to continue to exist . . . unless repairs to the *Klathas* outstrip our own. Until then . . ."

"Stalemate," Kirk decided, staring at the viewscreen.

On board the Klathas, Engineer Scott's counterparts were working furiously to remove twisted bits of metal, to cut away burned out components and circuitry so that the arduous task of replacing them could begin.

Kumara was there himself, surveying the damage. He moved easily among the destruction, accompanied by Engineer Korreg and Lieutenant Kritt, offering a word of encouragment here, a blistering insult there—whatever seemed appropriate to accelerate the work.

He thought of Kirk, and worried as he fumed. "It's not going fast enough, Korreg."

"I abase myself, Exalted Commander. My head is yours . . . but my technicians are working as fast as they are able. There is much structural damage. It must be removed, cut away, before actual repair can begin."

"I'll cut off some extremities if replacement of damaged instrumentation doesn't commence within a hundred *aines*, Engineer. Tell them that. Perhaps it will stimulate their muscles, if not their minds."

"I will tell them, Commander," and Korreg hastily departed from the vicinity of the commander.

Kumara turned suddenly on the attentive Lieutenant Kritt. Kritt cringed—needlessly, as it developed. The commander had started at a sudden thought, not from any desire to heap abuse on his subordinate.

"Have the human Delminnen brought from the restraining chamber to the bridge. I'll meet you there."

"At once, Commander." The lieutenant turned to go, then hesitated. "It may take a few moments to . . . ah . . . restore the human to presentability."

"So long as he's coherent and will remain so. And for the *Sequa*'s sake, tell those in charge of him that this is no ordinary human. He is a valuable property and is to be treated as such ... or I will match their living conditions and treatment on board with his."

"Yes, Commander." Kritt hurried down the corridor while Kumara made his thoughtful way back to the bridge.

As it turned out, Van Delminnen appeared well able to manipulate both body and mind, though the former was not undamaged. But Kumara's warning had been delivered. The two husky guards who half carried, half dragged the slight human onto the bridge handled him with appropriate care.

Delminnen shook himself free of his captors, who gladly let him go—the feel of the soft human being difficult to stomach. He glanced around the bridge, his head moving rapidly, quickly, like a bird hunting for an especially ripe bug in the bark of a tree. His gaze settled contemptuously on Kumara, who gazed back with interest.

Kritt moved angrily from his station to stand next to Delminnen. "Bow in the presence of the commander, weak one!"

Delminnen's head went back slightly, prompting Kritt to raise a furious fist.

But Kumara waved the lieutenant off. "No, no, no, Kritt! How many times must I tell you to utilize your head for something other than shoulder ballast? Leave the poor creature alone. In your justifiable anger you might accidentally mortally damage it. Then how would we obtain the information we seek? One cannot coerce a corpse. Return to your position and continue to monitor the *Enterprise*. That is where my concern lies—not with this single human."

"As you command, Exalted One," Kritt muttered disappointedly. "But the disrespect—" Throwing the imperturbable Delminnen a vicious smile, he turned and stalked back to his station.

Kumara waited until the lieutenant was seated. Then he clasped his hands together around one knee, leaned back slightly, and struggled to execute an earnest grin—which for a Klingon was no mean feat.

"Now then, Van Delminnen ... It has come to the

attention of the Empire that you have developed a device based on new scientific principles which seems capable of reducing normal worlds to collections of drifting debris. I hardly need impress upon you that we would regard the possession of such a device by a government unfriendly to ours as threatening in the extreme."

"Whereas," Delminnen countered sarcastically, "if it were given into your protection, everyone could rest assured that it would be used for the benefit of all."

"Naturally."

"You're a liar—and worse, an unimaginative one."

There was a violent bang as of flesh on metal and some loud murmurings behind Kumara at that unpardonable insult. The commander turned and barked sharply, "Officers of the *Klathas,* attend to your duties!" Then he turned back to Delminnen and continued to smile amiably.

"Very well, since you doubt our motives . . ."

"I don't doubt them one bit," Delminnen sneered.

". . . let me rephrase the situation. You must concede that the Federation would utilize your device for similar purposes should they gain control of it. They will offer you little in return. On the other hand, you are my prisoner. Rather than be disagreeable, if you turn over the plans for your device to us, I will swear on my ancestors that you and your sister will be safely—"

That promise brought a sign of concern from the human, whose steel exterior showed the first indications of cracking slightly.

"Char . . . she's on board too?"

"Why, certainly," Kumara admitted, with commendable swiftness. "You don't think we'd separate the two of you, did you?"

Delminnen looked understandably suspicious. "She wasn't with us when we materialized in your transporter."

"Naturally not," Kumara agreed, his mind working as fast as only Kirk knew it could. "The *Enterprise* tried to snatch both of you from us. To compensate, we had to use two transporters. Your sister boarded the *Klathas* in the other one."

"Then why haven't I seen her?"

"She experienced some minor injuries when materializing in an awkward position. At the moment she is resting quietly and comfortably in our infirmary chambers. My chief medical officer informs me that she can have visitors in another day.

"Of course, I don't *want* to keep you apart any longer than that, Van Delminnen. But if you insist on being obstinate, you'll discover that I am a master of obstinacy.

"Should you decide, logically, to cooperate, you will be provided with a luxurious and private abode in an environment of your own choosing. You will have the facilities of a fully equipped laboratory, all the materials you require, and a free hand to spend the rest of your lives carrying out any kind of research you desire. Your privacy will be guarded and assured, and within the limits of the Empire you can come and go as you wish. Anything else you desire you have only to request." His voice rose in an excellent imitation of hearty good fellowship.

"Come, come, man . . . would your own government offer you as much? Or would they put you off with a modest stipend and a warning to take care with what you study? What say you?"

Delminnen locked eyes with the commander. His reply was jerky, nervous, as was all of his speech, but there was a firmness to it nonetheless.

"I say it's mighty peculiar for you to be so accommodating and generous to the helpless prisoner from a race you despise. And if you were as confident of eventually obtaining the information you want, by one means or another, you wouldn't be so anxious to secure my agreement. I know the *Enterprise* has been following your ship." He crossed his arms with an air of finality. "I think I'll wait a bit before agreeing to anything. There are developments yet to be seen."

That was too much for Kritt. Despite Kumara's

order, he was out of his chair, all but snarling at this infuriating example of a lower order.

"Let me have him for a few *aines* in the persuasion chambers, Most Exalted. I'll show him the folly of attempting to dictate to a Klingon commander."

"Please, Lieutenant." Kumara sighed irritably. "I am conducting the interrogation. While I might agree with your desires, emotionally, your suggestion is premature. Have you not studied this creature? I have done so, while he has been babbling.

"While possibly a veritable genius, he is obviously, like so many of his kind, mentally unstable. Torture might send him into a catatonic state from which his mind—and the secrets locked therein—might never emerge.

"In that case, I would find it necessary to have the questioner—yourself, for example—executed. I should prefer not to. At times you have shown yourself to perform somewhat less incompetently than your compatriots. Do return to your station."

Thoroughly disgusted both with the situation and with the commander's attitude toward it, Kritt returned once again to his position. He sat there fuming quietly and thinking of what he would do to the human if he were in Kumara's place.

"Van Delminnen," Kumara said, "I cannot understand your attitude. Even for a human, it is exceptionally obtuse. Let us try this—a communication between yourself and Captain Kirk which we monitored earlier showed you emphatically refusing him even permission to land. If you hate him and the Federation he stands for, which has so grievously and wrongly mistreated you, why not spite them all by turning your knowledge over to us?"

Delminnen drew himself up in a self-conscious pose of pride and arrogance—a very Klingon thing to do, in fact. "My genius," he informed Kumara, "is not for sale to the highest bidder. You all desire my knowledge, yet none of you is sufficiently intelligent to know how to ask for it." He smiled in a strange way—strange even for him.

Kumara was mildly amused, but not by the smile. "You have a novel way of rationalizing your insanity, Delminnen. Too novel for me. I haven't the time to probe it just now. Rest assured that there will be time for everything." He looked to the guard on the scientist's left.

"Convey him to Karau in Humanoid Psychology—perhaps they can figure this one out. And tell them not to damage him beyond what is absolutely necessary."

"It shall be as you say, Commander," the guard replied. The guards took hold of Delminnen, despite his protests, and escorted him from the bridge.

Kumara turned thoughtfully back to the main viewscreen. He hadn't really expected the human to be sensible and agree to the inevitable. The only time his demeanor had altered was when his sibling had been mentioned. If she were on board now, it would be a simple matter to use her as a lever with which to topple Delminnen's stubbornness.

But she wasn't on board. She was out there, somewhere in the bowels of Kirk's ship, and Kumara did not think Kirk would be so foolish as to permit him access to her.

Still, he had Delminnen. It might take longer, be a bit messier, but eventually they would pry the information out of him—provided they all weren't vaporized first.

With his mind he tried to bridge the gap between ships, reach across to the tiny bump at the apex of the cruiser's saucer which he knew housed the ship's bridge. He reached out and tried to penetrate a single mind therein.

What are you thinking, acquaintance of my youth, he mused to himself. How will you proceed? We are even with our guesswork now. Whatever happens next could be decisive. Whence will it come, and when it does, will the gods permit me to escape again?

The trouble is, James Kirk, I know you too well—and you know me. How does one fool a mirror . . . ?

"I wonder what Kumara's thinking now, Bones."

Kirk's gaze remained fixed on the screen, which still showed the image of the damaged Klingon cruiser.

McCoy's reply was bitter: "Probably laughing himself silly over the way he suckered us into that last barrage. Sitting in his command chair, watching us bleed and snickering to himself."

"How are things in Sick Bay?" Kirk asked, aware that the anger was directed more at the result of Klingon bellicosity—the casualties the ship had suffered—than at Kumara himself.

"Better than we deserve, Jim. If the one projector that did most of the engine damage had struck at a broader angle instead of slant-on, we could have suffered a blood bath back there. As it is, there are half a dozen specialists and one ensign who'll be lucky to pull through."

"If they're not dead already, they never will be, Bones. Not with you hovering over them."

"I wish I had your confidence in me, Jim." He glanced down at his wrist chronometer. "She ought to be here by now. I told—"

"Captain . . . Dr. McCoy?" Both men turned to face the elevator.

Two people had just emerged. One was a medical specialist. The other was Char Delminnen. She looked pale but otherwise none the worse for her wrestling match with transporter energies. The resemblance to her brother, Kirk noted, was amazing. A few slight changes in bone structure here, a movement of skin, and they could have been twins.

She was looking with interest around the bridge. Eventually her gaze settled on Kirk, and she inspected him with the same thoroughness with which he had regarded her.

The specialist marched her over, saluted, and waited for McCoy's instructions.

"Report, Mendez."

"All vital signs strong, body functions normal. No evidence to indicate delayed-time reactions. Mental condition stable."

"All right, you can go, Mendez," McCoy told him.

"Tell Nurse Chapel to keep me posted if any of the casualties on critical show signs of deterioration."

"Yes, sir." The specialist saluted again and left the bridge, leaving Kirk and McCoy free to appraise Char Delminnen for the first time.

And they were in for a hard time, Kirk reflected, if she was anything like her brother.

"How do you feel, Ms. Delminnen?" McCoy ventured. Her gaze rested briefly on the doctor, then turned immediately to Kirk. He found her voice unexpectedly light, almost musical. But it was as adamantine as her brother's.

"Captain, where is Van?"

Kirk glanced for approval to McCoy, who nodded once. "She's as sound as I can make her, Jim. You might as well tell her."

Her attention shifted confusedly from McCoy to Kirk and back again. "What is this . . . what are you talking about? Isn't . . . isn't Van on board this ship?"

Kirk raised a placating hand and turned to indicate the screen. "I'm afraid I have to tell you he is not, Ms. Delminnen. Unless we're much mistaken, he's on that one."

They waited, McCoy watching her anxiously while she stared silently at the disabled Klingon cruiser. There was no scream, no violent outburst, not the slightest hint of hysteria. But her next words were whispered.

"I see. The Klingons got Van and you got me." She turned abruptly to look accusingly at Kirk. "Have you been in contact with them? Do you know if he's all right?"

"We've been in contact all right," Kirk explained patiently. "We've been fighting a running battle with them for much too long. Both our ship and the *Klathas* have been disabled. At the moment it's a race to see who can repair their engines first.

"As to your brother, we've had no word from the Klingons. They haven't volunteered any information, and we haven't had time to request any—not that they'd be inclined to make comments about anything other than our theoretical ancestry at the moment."

Char Delminnen turned her eyes to the deck and sighed. "Ever since our parents died and we were farmed out to foster parents, Van and I have never been separated for very long. We see things too much the same, too well, to look elsewhere for companionship." Her eyes turned up to him, and they were haunted.

"I don't know how he'll react if we're kept apart very long. In many ways Van is still a child. You've got to find a way to return him to me, Captain Kirk!"

The fury behind her request took both men aback. Though he had no reason to be ashamed of their efforts thus far, Kirk found himself squirming under that demanding gaze.

"We've been risking the ship and our lives to do just that, Ms. Delminnen. I don't think you need worry too much. Your brother's extremely important to the Klingons as well as to us. You can bet they're being careful not to harm him."

He did not think it would be diplomatic to discuss the ultimate steps they were prepared to take to keep Van Delminnen and his device from falling into the Empire's hands.

Char Delminnen relaxed physically at Kirk's assurance, but her words, as she turned away slightly, were still filled with fury . . . and bitterness.

"And all this has happened because of that stupid discovery of his. I told him some interloper might discover evidence of its use. I *told* him! But would he listen?" She shook her head slowly. "That child—the universe is his playpen." Her head snapped around, and Kirk found himself confronted by that accusing stare again.

"That's the only reason you're interested in us, isn't it? You're no better than the Klingons."

Kirk bridled. "I think we, and the Federation—*your* Federation, Ms. Delminnen, whether you like it or not—are entitled to better than that. As for personal concern, comparing us with the Klingons is akin to—"

"Yes, that is the reason," Spock interrupted. Kirk threw his first officer a look of reproach.

"Thank you, Mr. ... Spock, isn't it? I appreciate your honesty. At least I'm sure of where I stand."

"We could express more concern for you," Spock continued, looking up from the library computer console, "but you and your brother make it exceedingly difficult for anyone else to be interested in anything *but* your work."

Kirk's look of reproach vanished, and he saw that Char Delminnen had no reply to Spock's accusation. All she could do was shrug.

"So Van and I are jealous of our privacy. We didn't ask for visitors. We didn't inflict ourselves on you. It was the other way around."

"So it was," Kirk agreed firmly, "but you invited this visitation whether you'll admit it or not. Yes, our primary concern is the device—and why shouldn't it be? Do you realize what the Klingons will do, what they'll be able to demand, if they gain possession of a weapon so destructive that—"

"Oh, for heaven's sake, don't you understand?"

Kirk and McCoy looked at her askance. "What do you mean?"

"The device . . . it's not a weapon."

VIII

Clearly, there were those on the bridge whose attention was not focused solely on their tasks of the moment, for the general shock this comment produced spread beyond Kirk and McCoy.

"Wait . . . I think I understand you," Kirk finally began, speaking in a soothing, calming manner. "It's all a matter of semantics. Very possibly your brother did not regard his invention as a weapon. You must see, however, that to an outsider any device which is capable of obliterating an entire world . . ."

"Yes, yes . . . but you have to know, Captain Kirk, it was never conceived as a weapon. For all his intransigence, Van could no more develop a weapon of destruction than he could moderate a diplomatic conference."

"If destroying planets isn't an offensive gesture," wondered McCoy, "then what was this machine's intended purpose?"

"You know that this system is exceptionally poor in usable metals? That was a major reason why it was never colonized, not even outposted."

McCoy looked blank. "So?"

"Van got the idea for a device which would enable orbiting vessels to mine such metals at depths previously thought impossible, and from great distances. It involved the calculus of stress in ways I don't pretend to understand. I'm not sure anyone but Van could understand them.

"It sounded like a grandiose absurdity at first, but Van became obsessed with the thought. He neglected all our other projects, threw himself wholly into this one. You have no idea, gentlemen, what Van becomes when he is obsessed with an idea."

"I can imagine," ventured McCoy.

117

"He doesn't eat, he doesn't sleep—he exists to work. He exists *on* work. And eventually he produced the concepts needed to make the device a reality." Her grim visage lightened in remembrance. "How excited he was, how thrilled, how expectant! This was the discovery which was going to refute his critics. This was to bring him the recognition forever denied by petty, less talented men." She slumped.

"What else is there to say? You saw the results for yourselves. We tried the finished machine out on kilometers-deep nickel-iron deposits in the mantle of the ninth planet. The result was destructive beyond all imagining. Van was appalled, then furious . . . at the machine and at himself. He reworked, recalculated everything. He found no mistake. By his calculations, the machine should have worked as it was.

"I tried to dissuade him from making another test." She laughed disconsolately. "Try to extinguish a sun. So we aimed the machine at iridium deposits on the eighth world . . . with identical results.

"Do you wonder, Captain Kirk, Dr. McCoy, at the manner in which he greeted you? It was his failure infuriating him, not your presence. The latter he could stand, but not the first. That's why he refused to cooperate.

"But you've got to believe than Van intended no harm to anyone. He's no world-smashing monster. He wanted to produce something that would vindicate him, yes, but also to create something which would benefit Federation peoples." Abruptly the hard shell splintered and she was pleading.

"Get him back, Captain Kirk, please get him back! Without me he's no danger to anyone, except himself."

"Ms. Delminnen, while it may come as a shock to you, we *are* concerned about you and your brother in ways other than mercenary. As Federation citizens, and as individuals, it's our duty to protect you. Even if your brother had produced nothing of value, the mere fact that he's a Federation citizen would probably have impelled us along the same course of action we're following now."

"And after you've got him back, assuming you can do that . . . ?" she asked, in control of herself again.

"That will have to be decided by the Federation Council. I'm only a starship captain, you know—not the all-powerful manipulator of others' lives you seem to think I am."

She stared at him a moment longer. "Though I have absolutely no reason to do so, I find myself believing you, Captain Kirk. I realize, however, that you'll be forced to destroy the Klingon ship—and my brother— if you fail to recapture him."

Kirk looked surprised—he thought he had avoided the need to mention that final, fatal possibility altogether. He hadn't counted on this woman's perceptiveness—it was almost as if she'd read his mind.

"We don't intend . . ." he started to mumble, and then decided to be as forthright as she was. "You understand, then, that we simply cannot . . . *cannot* permit the Klingons to rebuild your brother's device."

Char Delminnen's reaction was unexpected. She was momentarily speechless with shock. "Oh, but don't you see . . . didn't you know?" she finally explained. "They *can't.*"

Now it was Kirk's turn to be shocked. The rest of the bridge was equally stunned. "Maybe you ought to elaborate," he said slowly.

She began to pace excitedly back and forth, waving one hand animatedly as she spoke. "I thought you had done your research, studied us thoroughly. It seems in your haste and anxiety to recover the weapon, both you and the Klingons neglected to trouble yourselves much with its creators. Yes," she half shouted, forestalling McCoy's unvoiced comment, "I said *creators.* You've no idea how Van worked, do you?"

Kirk glanced over at Spock, who looked blank and shook his head negatively, once. Char Delminnen turned smug.

"Van couldn't build a toy truck, let alone anything as complicated as that machine. I told you how close we are. We always work together. Don't you remember me telling you that he was neglecting our projects?

Ours! Van gets an idea into his head, spins it around, clarifies the theory—and then I draw the diagrams and execute the finished product. He conceives, I construct. It has always been like that.

"After all, I'm the one with the degree in practical engineering."

"Mr. Spock?" Kirk eyed his first officer expectantly, but Spock was already working at the library computer. Shortly he turned and spoke softly.

"Historical records confirm the body of Delminnen's report."

"I see." He turned his attention back to the still-pacing woman. "What you're saying, then, is that your brother is incapable of duplicating the machine?"

"Duplicating! They couldn't construct a primitive crystal set from Van's instructions! I'm the only one who can understand his verbal and mathematical shorthand. The two of us make one genius, Captain. Separated, we're merely two competent technicians."

Kirk turned thoughtfully to the viewscreen and studied the still driveless *Klathas.* Soon he began to chuckle. The sound rose, concurrent with Spock's eyebrows, became a chortle, then a laugh.

"Jim!" McCoy stared at his friend. Spock was equally puzzled.

"Really, Captain. I hardly consider the information the young lady has recently imparted of such a nature as to—"

"I'm . . . sorry, Spock . . . Bones." He regained control of himself. "Forgive me, Ms. Delminnen. I wasn't laughing at your brother's plight, or at your concern. It's just so . . . so . . . I can't help but visualize Commander Kumara's expression when he pulls what you've just told us out of your brother, when he discovers that in all this haste and confusion, he's the one who should be chasing *us!*"

The situation they were now in suddenly dawned on McCoy. He too chuckled. Spock reguarded this display of emotion coolly.

Almost as coolly as did Char Delminnen: "I'll be in the cabin Dr. McCoy assigned to me, Captain. If and when you have additional questions, or have rescued my brother, you'll find I'm available."

She turned and marched pompously to the elevator. Kirk turned to McCoy.

"You're going to leave her to herself, Bones?"

"She's as healthy as I can make her, Jim. She and her brother may both need treatment, but not of a physical variety." He shook his head slowly. "What a family ... so much talent enveloped in so many neuroses."

Kirk turned and saw the rest of the bridge crew listening attentively. "What are you all staring at? Don't you have stations to man? In case some of you aren't aware of it, this ship is on red alert and in the midst of an ongoing battle. Or perhaps there are some among you who ..."

The level of activity on the bridge rose rapidly.

"Mr. Spock, your estimation of how soon repairs to the *Klathas* will be completed?" The first officer bent to his console. He looked up calmly several moments later.

"It is difficult to evaluate the damage to the enemy vessel with much accuracy, Captain. Judging from the information available through the library, combined with that obtained by our sensors, however, I should say that they will complete minimally necessary repairs to their engines well ahead of us."

Kirk double-checked with Engineering and found that Scott confirmed Spock's analysis.

"All right, Scotty, do what you can. Kirk out." The captain sat back and considered their situation. If the *Klathas* were allowed to run under warp-drive for even a short time while the *Enterprise* remained comparatively immobile, they would lose contact with her completely. There had to be some way to prevent that. Phasers and photon-torpedo banks were inoperable owing to the damaged firecontrol computer; impulse power would be useless ... they had to stick with the *Klathas* somehow.

Stick with ...

"Mr. Arex."

"Yes Captain?" The Edoan navigator responded promptly.

"I need a report on the status of the tractor beams."

"Just a moment, sir." Arex checked his console, tried a few switches, and found they responded as programmed. "Instruments indicate that all tractor units are intact and capable of full function, sir. Power leads to Engineering are undamaged, and all other subsidiary instrumentation appears functional."

"Thank you, Mr. Arex." Down went the intercom button. "Scotty . . ."

"Aye, Captain, what now?" the chief engineer wondered. "If it's about the drive . . ."

"Not this time, Scotty. How would it affect your repair work back there if I had to request maximum, sustained power to the tractor beams?"

"The tractors?" Scott hesitated only long enough to mentally retrace one diagram out of several thousand locked and filed securely in the manual of his mind. "Not at all, Captain. That's an independent power link. I can give you all the attractive force you want."

"I'll hold you to that, Scotty," Kirk told him thankfully. "We may need it all." He clicked off and snapped an order to the helm. "Mr. Sulu! Prepare to engage the *Klathas* with all forward tractors. Use near full power, one unit below maximum."

"Aye, sir," Sulu responded. "Should I attempt to close the distance between us?"

"Negative, Mr. Sulu. Maintain present disposition. We're close enough for effective tractor work. I don't want to move in to where Kumara can use portable weaponry against us. Since we can't go anywhere until Mr. Scott's people have repaired the drive, I just want to make sure the Klingons can't go anywhere without us."

"Prepared to lock onto enemy vessel, Captain," Sulu reported. "All forward tractors powered and standing by."

"Engage, Mr. Sulu."

The helmsman gave the necessary electronic order.

There was the briefest pause before a slight quiver was felt on the bridge.

A jolt was felt on the bridge of the *Klathas*. Kumara looked up as Kritt reported, "Commander, sensors indicate that the Federation vessel has—"

"Locked onto us with her tractor beams," Kumara finished for him. "I don't require mechanicals to confirm that for me. It was an obvious desperation move." He eyed the drifting *Enterprise*. "I only wonder why it took them so long."

Five *aines* passed before Kumara's chair intercom buzzed for attention. "Report yourself," he said to the pickup.

"Engineering here, Exalted Commander." There was a touch of exultation in Korreg's exhausted voice. "I am pleased to report that we have restored partial drive capability."

A shrill battle cry broke out on the bridge at these words. For once Kumara decided to ignore the breach of discipline. The men could do with a little enthusiasm.

"Remember, Commander, we have only partial capability. Our speed and maneuverability are still severely limited."

"I understand, Korreg. It will be enough, I think. My commendation to you and your personnel. At the successful completion of this mission there will be honors for all. I salute you."

He turned from the intercom to an uncertain Kritt. "But, Exalted One, there is still the problem of the *Enterprise*'s tractors."

"Must I constantly be afflicted with reminders of the obvious?" Kumara moaned. "Am I forever to be oppressed by relentless idiocy? Worm's offspring, product of a misaligned mating, can you see no solution to anything save what is written already? Prepare to get under way!"

"At once, Commander!" a rejuvenated Kritt responded. The rest of the bridge crew bent to their own tasks happily, secure in the confidence expressed by their commander's renewed good mood.

Sulu's attention was caught by the sudden activation of long-quiescent readouts. "Captain," he announced anxiously, "the *Klathas* appears to be increasing speed."

"Confirmed, Captain," Spock declared evenly. "They are approaching velocity beyond the ability of impulse power. It would seem that they have their warp-drive working again."

"Mr. Sulu," Kirk inquired, "report on the status of all tractor linkages."

The helmsman hurriedly checked the appropriate telltales and reported steadily, "Tractors all holding firm, sir. No sign of weakening, and all instrumentation operating efficiently."

"Mr. Spock, compute energy output of the *Klathas* and compare with her rate of acceleration." Spock did the necessary figuring and announced a figure. Kirk relaxed a little. "They've regained only partial use of their drive, Spock. By the time they can complete their repairs, according to your estimates of the damage they've suffered, Mr. Scott should have restored our own engines back to equal operation. That means full use of our weapons systems as well, since the firecontrol computer is expected to be fixed at the same time." He looked satisfied.

"Then we can restart this argument on an equal basis again . . ."

Lieutenant Kritt looked up from his console, some of his initial enthusiasm at the return of drive capability now dampened by what his readouts told him.

"We are approaching warp-speed, Commander, but we cannot exceed it by much until further repairs have been completed by Engineering. We do not have enough power to break the *Enterprise*'s tractor lock on us."

Kumara remained relaxed, confident. "Not with sheer speed we do not, Lieutenant."

"Your pardon, Exalted One?"

"Pay attention, Kritt." Kumara's voice rose to reach every attentive ear on the bridge. "Pay attention, all of you. We will execute the following course changes, and execute them with utmost precision. And in so doing, we will finish this absurd contest once and for all . . ."

There was no panic on the *Enterprise*'s bridge when evidence of the initial Klingon maneuver was reported by her detectors.

"Captain," Sulu declared promptly, "the Klingons are shifting strongly to starboard, running at a considerable angle now to their previous course."

I wonder what Kumara is up to, Kirk thought.

"It seems strange, Captain," Spock announced, obviously puzzled. "They have the benefit, however temporary, of warp-drive capability. I should think their proper course of action would be to make as much distance toward their base at Shahkur as possible before we regain use of our own drive and weapons."

"I agree, Spock. That's my thought too. Possibly Kumara is trying to trick us again, trying to convince us there's Klingon aid closer but in a different direction." He began to be concerned. It wasn't like Kumara to try anything so transparent.

"Mr. Spock, you're certain the Klingons have no military facilities nearer than Shahkur?"

Spock utilized the library briefly. "Absolutely nothing, Captain. Shahkur is at the extreme fringe of the Empire. And the Klingons do not normally patrol this region in force, so I think it extremely unlikely they have contacted another ship."

"He's up to something," Kirk muttered.

At that moment a slight quiver ran through the bridge. "*Klathas* has executed another radical course change, Captain," Sulu reported. "Approximately forty-five degrees to port of their new course."

"Tractor status?"

"Still holding tight, Captain," Arex announced quietly. "We're staying with them. No change in disposition."

Another quiver rattled the bridge. It was slightly stronger this time.

Sulu's voice rose slightly. "Now they're shifting to starboard again."

On the screen Kirk saw the *Klatha*s nearly vanish to the right before scanner compensators realigned her in the center of the screen. Simultaneously, a strong jolt rocked the bridge so hard that Uhura had to grab the arms of her chair to keep from being thrown free.

"Shifting again, Captain!"

"Steady, Mr. Sulu." He was on the intercom instantly. Now it was obvious what Kumara was up to. The question was . . . could they do anything about it?

"Scotty, have you restored any drive capability yet? Anything at all?"

"No, Captain," the chief engineer replied. "And"— his voice was momentarily drowned out as the next shock rocked the *Enterprise* and forced Kirk to brace himself against the arm of the chair—"we're not goin' to have any if this infernal shakin' gets any worse. What the devil's goin' on up there?"

"It's the Klingon ship. Kumara knows he hasn't regained enough power to break free of our tractors, so he's playing crack-the-whip . . . with us on the snapping end."

"The colloquial identification is obscure, Captain," Spock firmly declared, "but the physical theory cannot be quarreled with. If this continues, the centripetal force will soon be sufficient to overpower our tractor beams and break the *Klathas* free."

Kirk didn't have to cut the intercom—the next shock did that. This one was severe enough to send sparks flying from several consoles and knock two momentarily unbraced specialists to the deck.

McCoy stumbled over to the command chair and grabbed the back for support. "Jim, we can't go on like this. If it gets any worse, it won't matter whether the Klingons break free or not. I'm receiving injury reports already, from all over the ship." Another jolt sent him spinning to the floor, despite his hold on the chair back.

"Captain, I must concur with the doctor," Spock insisted, struggling to retain his own position. "Calculations indicate that much additional stress will begin to affect the ship's hull. Even the strongest seams cannot take—"

"All right, Spock!" Kirk's mind churned furiously. There was no time for careful consideration of possible alternatives, no time to judge possible reciprocal effects of his idea.

Besides, it was his only idea. The trouble was, it could affect them as severely as it did the Klingons.

Another shock struck as the *Klathas* slammed over to a new heading once more. The tractors still held, a credit to their designers. Unfortunately, human beings were not nearly so solidly constructed.

Kirk climbed painfully back into the command chair, every millimeter of his body bruised and strained. Only Arex, with his triple limbs, had succeeded in retaining his position during that last shock, but even he appeared shaken.

Lights flickered momentarily, then came on strong. The next time they might not. "Mr. Spock, I want a half-second countdown to the *Klathas*'s next projected course change. They have to maintain a set pattern of changes for maximum effectiveness."

"Fifteen, fifteen, fourteen, fourteen . . ." Spock recited in a monotone, not questioning the reasoning behind the command.

"Mr. Arex, on command you will disengage tractor beams for the minimum amount of time possible, then reengage. Do you understand?"

"No, sir . . . but standing ready." One finger hovered over the button in question, still with inhuman control.

". . . Nine, nine, eight, eight . . ." The first officer continued to count, his voice never wavering.

"Stress on the exterior plates is nearing the danger point, sir," the ensign at the engineering station reported tensely. Kirk ignored him, his gaze locked on the screen, where the *Klathas* was sliding rapidly to starboard again, his attention focused on Spock's count to the exclusion of all else.

". . . Four, four, three, three, two, two . . ."

"Whatever you're going to do, Jim, *do* it!" yelled McCoy.

". . . One, o—"

"Now, Arex!"

The Edoan's finger descended, firmly depressed the switch controlling the forward tractors, allowed it to rise, then depressed it again. The action was almost too fast for a human eye to follow.

Several things happened at once. A tiny dial on Arex's console barely quivered. A tremendous force wrenched at the *Enterprise*. It sounded as though every bit of metal—every plate, beam, wire, down to the fillings in Scott's back teeth—vibrated in protest. This time the lights stayed out. The only illumination on the bridge was provided by the brilliant display of sparks which arced from one outraged console to another.

Transparent facings on gauges and dials shattered, and everyone, including Arex, was thrown heavily to the deck.

Kirk had only a glimpse of the screen as he was thrown clear of the command chair. It dimmed but didn't wink out entirely. It showed the *Klathas* whipping around like a top, to stop facing the *Enterprise* bow-on.

The lights came back on slowly, but with none of the usual crispness of emergency backups snapping in. Groans and mild curses, indicative of pain incurred, formed a slowly rising murmur on the bridge.

Kirk had to pull himself bodily back into his chair. "Mr. Arex, report," he said, wincing and clutching at his right shoulder. "Report on the status of the Klingon vessel. Disposition and speed relative to our own."

There was a long pause. This time not even Arex had escaped the pounding, and it took a few minutes for the Edoan's jarred mind to settle enough so that he could make sense of what his instruments were telling him—those that were still operative.

"Instruments show . . . instruments show . . ." His soulful eyes widened slightly in surprise. "Sir, all engine activity, including impulse power, has ceased aboard the *Klathas!*"

"Mr. Spock, confirmation." *Please*, he added silently.

"Correct, Captain," the first officer reported. "The *Klathas* shows no evidence of internal power beyond what is required to maintain vital life-support systems. She shows no signs of drive activity."

"And what about ourselves?"

Spock studied his instrumentation a moment longer. "We have apparently sustained additional damage as well, Captain. We are in little better shape than the *Klathas.*"

"Damage reports starting to come in, Captain," Uhura announced. Her left cheek was swollen and badly discolored, but her voice was as crisp and precise as ever.

"Make note of them, Lieutenant," Kirk responded, "and I'll review them at first opportunity. Meanwhile, get me Engineering."

Uhura worked her console, then explained, "Sorry, sir . . . that portion of intership communications is presently inoperative. Lieutenant M'ress has checked in to say that she is working on the breakdown with communications personnel and Engineering Maintenance."

"It may be just as well, Jim," McCoy suggested. "I'm not sure I'd care to listen to Scotty just now—not after what that last shock must have done to his half-finished repairs. What *did* happen, anyway?"

"It worked is what happened, Bones, although it worked on both of us—on the *Enterprise* as well as on the *Klathas.*" He tried to slip into a comfortable position, discovered that his battered body found no position comfortable, and tried to take his mind off the throb in his shoulder by explaining.

"Did you ever play crack-the-whip when you were a kid, Bones? On any kind of skates?"

"Sure." He grimaced. "I always seemed to end up on the outside end."

"What would happen if that outside end suddenly grabbed hold of something immovable, like a fixed post or other solid object, and held on—even if only for a second?"

McCoy's brows drew together in thought. Then he smiled and nodded slowly. "Of course ... The shock would be transmitted all the way down the line, to the inner end. If it were done to a line of skating kids, the ones at the other end would be shaken off ... although everyone would experience the shock to some degree." His eyes suddenly moved to the screen. "So that's what happened to the *Klathas*." He gestured at the now completely immobile alien ship. "It spun them completely around. And I thought *we'd* taken the worst of it."

"Jubilation is pleasant but only temporary, Doctor," Spock suggested unexcitedly, calmly—rationally. He turned his gaze to Kirk. "What do we do now, Captain?"

"Now?" Kirk spread his upturned palms in an age-old gesture. "I'm afraid I didn't have much time to think about that, Mr. Spock. We had to cope somehow, and it seems we have. Do now?" He looked up at the screen.

"We wait to see who can repair his engines or phasers first. Until then, both vessels will continue to drift along exactly as we are—eye to eye, nose to nose—calling each other bad names."

"A most unprofitable apportionment of mental resources, Captain," the first officer observed disapprovingly.

"What was that, Spock?"

"Pay no attention, Jim," McCoy advised him. "Spock's just jealous because Vulcans are culture-conditioned against swearing."

"Word inebriation," Spock countered, slightly miffed. But that was the end of it ...

IX

"Captain's log, supplemental." Kirk paused, took a long breath, and regarded the *Klathas*. Its position had not changed since Kumara's ploy to break free of the *Enterprise*'s tractors had been so joltingly countered. It still faced the *Enterprise* nose-on, the lights on its bridge glaring at the starship's scanners.

"We have been drifting below warp-speed together with the *Klathas* for several standard days now. Events have devolved into a race between the engineering complements of both vessels, to see which can be the first to effect repairs to their respective drives and offensive-weapons systems.

"Since phaser instrumentation requires considerably more time and effort, we are concentrating our efforts on repairing the warp-drive, with reasonable assurance that the Klingons are doing the same . . . or so Mr. Spock assures me, based on evidence of detectable activity on board the Imperial cruiser." He paused.

"My only consolation in all of this," he finally concluded, "is the knowledge that Commander Kumara of the *Klathas* is probably more frustrated than I . . ."

He finished the log entry and switched the recorder off, then took the moment of relative quiet to survey the bridge. Spock was engaged in some esoteric research of his own, his instruments set to alert him to any hint of unusual activity on board the Klingon ship. Sulu was replaying a game of trifence on an auxiliary monitor, his own telltales quiet. Uhura was half asleep at her console.

Only Arex appeared alert and absorbed. Come to think of it, the navigator had remained attentive to something for several hours now.

"What do you find so interesting, Mr. Arex?" Kirk asked.

"Hmmm?" The delicate head with its jutting bony ridges turned, limpid eyes gazed back at Kirk. "I have been engrossed in the approach of an impossibility, Captain."

Spock showed that he wasn't all that buried in research by turning to listen curiously. "Elucidate, Lieutenant."

"I have been debating whether to do precisely that, sir," Arex replied. "I wished to be certain of my findings first. It grows more extraordinary as we near. Even so, because of the uncertain situation with regard to the enemy vessel, I have hesitated before mentioning it."

"Before mentioning what, Mr. Arex?" wondered Kirk in puzzlement.

"Captain, my instruments indicate that we are approaching an object of planetary mass. Furthermore—and this is most exciting—it appears to possess free water in oceanic quantities and a breathable atmosphere."

Slowly the rest of the bridge began to stir from somnolence, began to utilize long-inactive instrumentation.

"Spock, the charts for this area—"

"Show it as an empty region, Captain. No stars, most certainly no planets." He bent to his gooseneck viewer, adjusted controls, made demands on exterior scanners and sensors. "Yet I must confirm Mr. Arex's observations." He looked up again, his eyes glowing with the fervor of a scientist who has just made a discovery as spectacular as it was unexpected.

" 'Extraordinary' is an understatement, Captain. It is unique."

"What's unique?" McCoy asked, strolling from the elevator. He had just concluded his tour of all the patients remaining in Sick Bay and satisfied himself as to their condition.

Kirk's voice was hushed with wonder. "We're apparently going to encounter a habitable world, Bones."

McCoy's gaze went to the viewscreen. It still showed only the *Klathas,* floating against a background of thinly sprinkled stars. And since the warp-drive was still out . . .

"A world . . . where, Jim? If we're approaching a sun, the scanners seem to be ignoring it."

"That's just it, Bones. There is no sun. We're going to meet a wanderer."

McCoy was properly startled. "A wanderer? An inhabitable wanderer? I thought such a thing was impossible, Jim."

"So did I, Bones. Any reasonable astronomer will tell you that the odds of encountering a planet which has broken free of its parent sun are . . . well, astronomical. I know of only two such encounters in Federation history, and both are well documented. This is a new discovery.

"But the chances of finding a wandering world with a breathable atmosphere, and free water on the surface . . ."

"Are beyond computation, Captain," Spock concurred. "I would not have believed it possible."

"To spot a non-system object of less than solar mass in free space, Bones, a ship has to be traveling below warp-one, on impulse power or less. No one travels like that . . . unless they've had an accident. Even then, with such incredible odds . . . Bones, this discovery is nearly as important as freeing Delminnen from the Klingons."

"I'm not sure Char Delminnen would agree with you, Jim," McCoy murmured softly.

Days passed. The *Enterprise* and the *Klathas*, locked together in mutual impotence, drifted closer to the wanderer. It grew from a statistic in Arex's computer to a ball, then to a globe, and finally to a massive, real world with continents and oceans and clouds.

Those clouds were the key to its habitability, for they were just thick enough to retain the heat the planet appeared to produce, yet not thick enough to produce a radical, suffocating greenhouse effect.

"According to sensors, the wanderer is about the same size as Earth," Spock was reporting, studying his readouts, "though its gravity is slightly stronger. Both the *Klathas* and the *Enterprise* have already been drawn into orbit around it."

"It's rich in heavy metals and radioactives, too," Kirk mused. "We already know it produces energy. At least we'll have the chance to inspect a unique spatial phenomenon at close range."

"And be carried a little bit farther from the Klingon base at Shahkur Nine while we're inspecting," McCoy pointed out with satisfaction.

"There's . . . there's something else, Captain," Spock reported. There was an odd note in the first officer's voice that made Kirk turn quickly.

"What is it, Mr. Spock?"

"Incredible as it may seem," he informed the bridge, his expression as close to stunned amazement as it was possible for it to be, "this wanderer appears to be not merely habitable, but inhabited."

Spock's astonishment was instantly transmitted to everyone on the bridge.

"Spock . . . you're certain?" Kirk finally managed to mumble.

"I don't think there is any question of it, Captain. There is too much evidence for it to be denied, despite the uncertainty of high-resolution sensors. Roads, population density . . . all appear present, though in very limited fashion. It suggests a well-populated world, though a technologically impoverished one. Actual surface survey may reveal otherwise, of course."

McCoy was staring at the brilliant, glistening cloud layer against which the *Klathas* was outlined. "What must they be like, Jim, a people who have developed never knowing a sun or a moon—never even knowing the stars? If Spock's assessment of their progress is correct, they can't possibly have telescopes capable of piercing their protective cloud layer."

"I can't imagine a civilization maturing under these conditions, Bones. And yet"—Kirk gestured at the screen—"we're confronted with the actuality. What," he wondered, "should we call it?"

"That's easy, Jim. There's only one name for it—Gypsy."

For a change, Spock and the doctor were in perfect agreement.

Detailed charting of the wanderer began, under the auspices of Spock's science staff. At no time did anyone forget that a battle for survival could erupt with the *Klathas* at any moment, but Kirt could see no reason why nonessential personnel should not take the opportunity to make a thorough study of the wanderer, at least until hostilities resumed. Undoubtedly, the Klingons' science section was occupied by similar activities.

"Final estimates show gravity as one point fourteen Earth normal, atmosphere point ninety-six Earth-Vulcan normal at the surface, temperature in the temperate zones varying between one hundred eighty and two hundred five degrees K."

"Why would it vary?" McCoy asked. "There's no sun to warm any part of the globe more than another."

"The atmosphere is slightly heavier at the planet's equator, thinner at its poles," Spock explained, "although nowhere as extreme climatically as on Earth. There are no ice caps, for example. Other than that," the first officer finished, "this world is a near duplicate of Earth or Vulcan."

"What about light?" McCoy persisted. "How could any civilization develop in the total absence of light?"

"I could make a case for several such civilizations, Doctor, but for this remarkable world it is unnecessary. The dense atmosphere contains an extremely high proportion of ionized gases and natural fluorescents, which are excited by the abundance of radioactives in the surface. If anything, these people must be afflicted with perpetual illumination, and not darkness."

"I see." McCoy nodded. "They live under the granddaddy of all auroras."

"As to what the inhabitants are like, Doctor," Spock continued, "there is evidence—evidence which can be confirmed only by on-surface inspection—that they are at least roughly humanoid in appearance and build. We've sent down a few drone probes for close-in study.

Superficially, at least, the resemblance to the normal Vulcan-human pattern is astounding."

"Absolutely no chance of their being advanced enough to help in repairing the *Enterprise*, or in countering the Klingons?" a hopeful Kirk queried.

"I'm afraid not, Captain," Spock replied drily. "First impressions have only just been confirmed by the probes. There are no centers of population larger than a good-sized town. Settlement appears to be primarily rural, with even villages isolated and scattered. I would say they are in the process of emerging from a medieval era into one of primitive middle-class capitalism. I'd place their level of technology no higher than fifteenth-century Earth or fifth-epoch Vulcan."

"Then we're not likely to encounter warp-drive technicians awaiting our call for assistance," Kirk observed. "Even so, the fact that they've achieved any kind of civilization at all—the very fact of their existence—is incredible. What a pity that we're too busy fighting the Klingons to remain to study them."

Spock agreed sadly. "Most unfortunate, Captain. We can plot this world's position and a probable trajectory for it, but it will still be extremely difficult to locate again."

"Excuse me, Captain." Kirk turned his attention to Uhura. "We're being beamed from the *Klathas*."

"They've got their communications working again, then. Put it on the screen, Lieutenant."

Surprisingly, Kirk found he felt no particular animosity toward the figure who appeared. There were signs of strain on the man's face: indications of fatigue induced by too much worry and too little sleep.

Kirk wondered if he looked as bad.

"Good day to you, James Kirk," Kumara began pleasantly. "I trust you are feeling well?"

"I'm getting by, Kumara. Yourself?"

The Klingon commander frowned, appeared petulant. "I've been rather restless lately, I'm afraid. For one thing, I am still rearranging my quarters. That little trick of yours in cutting your tractors and then reestablishing contact after we had changed our course drastically realigned that section of the *Klathas*."

"Sorry to hear it," Kirk replied, in a tone which indicated he wasn't sorry at all. "I'll bet that's not the only thing that's had to be rearranged." For some reason, Kirk found this falsely jovial atmosphere quite irritating. Maybe it was the memory of the faces he had seen in Sick Bay these past days.

"All right, Kumara, you didn't break battle silence for the first time in days to apprise me of the state of your bedroom. What do you want?"

Kumara's outward demeanor wasn't shaken. He remained unruffled. "You are quite correct, Jim. You see, a new development has caused me to reconsider our position.

"I have only just discovered that the man Delminnen is utterly incapable of building, designing, or instructing my technicians in how to duplicate his awesome device. It appears only his female sibling can do that."

"You damned torturer!" McCoy exploded. "How did you pry that out of him, Kumara? I know the Klingons are noted for their inventiveness with—"

Kumara waved him to silence. "Please, ah,"—he peered harder at his own screen—"Doctor, I believe. Am I a barbarian, to resort to the primitive physical intimidation of helpless prisoners? Besides, I would not risk losing forever the knowledge held in the human Delminnen's mind.

"No, to be quite truthful, the human bragged about it all over the *Klathas* as soon as he became convinced his sibling was not on board. It was hardly necessary to pry anything out of him." The Klingon commander's expression twisted. "Needless to say, I viewed his revelation with considerable dismay."

Kirk was growing impatient. "All this unnatural courtesy and politeness must be upsetting your liver, Kumara. Why did you beam me? What is it you want?"

Kumara looked back at Kirk with exaggerated surprise. "Why, the same thing you do, Jim. An end to all this suspense and a final disposition of our ... um ... mutual interests."

"We'll settle that as soon as my chief engineer informs me our drive is repaired—which should be any minute now."

"Perhaps," Kumara admitted, smiling easily. "Then again, it may be some time yet before the damage to either of our ships is rectified. I have thought of another way."

"Careful, Jim," McCoy whispered.

"What *other* way, Kumara?"

"I propose a contest."

"A contest?" Kirk echoed warily. "What kind of contest?"

"One that is simple and effective." Kumara leaned forward. "It should appeal to you, Jim."

"Go on."

"It's simple, really. You wish the man Delminnen returned to you. I need his sibling. Separately, they are useless to both of us."

"I disagree," countered Kirk. "They're both still alive ... something they probably wouldn't be if you had both of them for very long."

"You question my morality, too, but never mind," Kumara continued. "Here is what I propose. I am sure you have been studying the extraordinary world below us intensively these past days. Each of us will assume the attire of the inhabitants. We will take one officer with us from our respective crews. You will also take the girl with you, while I shall bring the man.

"We will take nothing but these clothes, our communicators, and some local means of exchange, and we will beam down to the planet. There are methods of insuring that each side descends with the correct number of people, the right people, and nothing in the way of modern weapons. Neither side can attempt to unexpectedly beam the other aboard his ship, since we will both have transporters locked on us at all times. And you will recall what interlocking transporter fields did the *last* time."

"Jim, he's crazy," McCoy whispered anxiously. "You can't possibly be thinking of—"

"Go on, Kumara," Kirk said slowly.

"Each group of three will beam down at opposite ends of the largest town on the main continent, the one bordering the central sea where the two rivers meet. We will then allow ourselves three time periods under the local conditions to ... ah ... effect a determination of our conflict, one way or the other. If at the conclusion of that period a solution has not been achieved, each party will beam back up to its ship and we will try something else.

"Even if my group proves successful, it may still be that your ship will regain its drive and weapons capabilities first. Then my success will have been for naught. Naturally the reverse may occur. So in any case this may not necessarily be the resolution of our situation.

"What do you think?"

McCoy was stunned, for it seemed that Kirk was actually seriously considering the Klingon's proposal. "Jim, you're not thinking of going along with this madness, are you? Don't you see what he's up to? It's you he's worried about, not the *Enterprise*. He's thought up this entire bizarre scheme as a way of eliminating *you*."

"Quiet, Bones" was all Kirk said. To Kumara he explained, "I agree that we can insure through various means that no advanced weapons are transported down, that the number of personnel is limited to a single assisting officer, and so on. But even the best of such guarantees can be circumvented. I want something more."

Kumara looked like a man forced to play his last ace instead of holding it in reserve. "Very well." He rose from his command chair and lifted both arms in a peculiar salute that was half military, half religious in origin.

"I swear as commander of a warship of the Imperial Fleet, as a Klingon lord, by the sacred warrior's soul of his Imperial Majesty Emperor Karhammur the Fortieth, and by the God of Gods, Great Kinkuthanza, to abide by the terms of the contest I have just set before us and before witnesses."

He lowered his arms and resumed his seat. "Furthermore, I agree to exchange ships' *nadas*. They will be able to oversee the actual transporting of each group to the surface, besides acting as hostages."

Kirk considered, ignoring McCoy's silent entreaties. The stalemate was unnerving. Should the Klingons finish their repairs first, he would be at a decided disadvantage. He looked across at Spock and saw his first officer waiting patiently.

"What's your opinion, Mr. Spock?"

"I am not qualified to offer an opinion where a superior officer's life is at stake, Captain. However, I believe the commander's suggestion could be turned to our advantage."

Kirk nodded. "My thoughts exactly, Spock."

McCoy looked angrily over at the first officer. "You're crazy too, Spock! What makes you think a Klingon's going to adhere to any kind of rules?"

"Two things, Bones. First of all, Spock, can you recall any instance of a Klingon officer's breaking an oath sworn on the Emperor's soul and on Kinkuthanza?"

"Never, Captain. To do so would be the equivalent of murdering one's honor, and the honor of one's line back to the first generation. It is one of the few things I can think of which would be binding on a Klingon."

"Kumara," Kirk said curtly, turning back to the screen, "I accept your proposal."

"Excellent! I will beam down with one assisting officer to the eastern end of the town, the sector known to the inhabitants as 'Gray Shadow,' in one hour, your time, from the cessation of this conversation. You were always first in classes at the FEA in Adaptive Ecology, Jim. You will be a challenge. Rest assured the human Delminnen will be with me." His arms came up and crossed again in that peculiar fashion.

"Good hunting, Jim."

The screen blanked. "Transmission ended, Captain," Uhura reported.

Kirk activated the intercom. "Alien Ecology and Sociology, attention. This is the captain speaking. I will require in forty minutes suitable attire for myself, Science Lieutenant Bresica Celli, and Ms Char Delminnen for a stay on the surface of Gypsy. Nothing fancy—you should aim for clothing appropriate for members of the lower noble classes. Also an ample supply of the local medium of exchange. Simulations must be accurate enough to fool the locals."

As he broke off and rose from the chair, McCoy stepped between Kirk and the elevator. "You're not going through with this, Jim. There are more sensible ways to get yourself killed!"

"What makes you think I'm the one who's going to get killed, Bones? I'm afraid I've got to take the risk. Kumara's gambling too. This may be our only chance to rescue Van Delminnen. If we finish engine and weapons repairs first, you know they're going to kill him rather than risk the Federation's obtaining the device. But if we conclude our repairs first *and* have both Delminnens safely on board ... no, I can't pass up that chance."

McCoy looked desperately over at the science station. "Spock, you reason with him!"

Spock left his position and confronted Kirk, who looked back at him in surprise. "I fear the doctor is correct, Captain. I must object. As it stands now, this scheme is inadvisable, highly dangerous, and illogical."

"There, you see?" McCoy looked satisfied.

"What's the matter, Spock?" a puzzled Kirk wondered. "A moment ago you declared the contest could be to our advantage. What's made you change your mind?"

"He's seen reason, that's all, Jim."

Spock's brows arched as he glanced at McCoy. "I always see reason, Doctor." Spock turned to face Kirk. "It is your present choice of personnel, Captain, which prompts my objection."

Kirk frowned. The frown turned into a grin, and he walked back to the command chair and activated the intercom. "Sciences? Inform Lieutenant Celli his services will not be required on this expedition. The second set of native clothing should conform to the uniform specifications of First Officer Spock." He cut off and smiled back over his shoulder.

"Mr. Spock?"

Not a sign of a smile cracked that stolid visage, not a hint of a chuckle modulated the reply, but Kirk sensed both nonetheless.

"I withdraw my objection, Captain. Subsequent modifications now indicate that participation in the contest is logical."

"Spock!"

The first officer turned a reproving gaze on McCoy. "As the captain is determined to go, Doctor, it is only sensible that the best-qualified support accompany him. I am the best-qualified support. Therefore, I am going too. Really, you complicate things unnecessarily."

Spock brushed by a dazed McCoy, following Kirk into the elevator.

Alien Sociology was in constant communication with the engineers in Nonmetallic Fabrication, with the result that Kirk had hardly entered his cabin when a specialist, laden with an armload of clothing, buzzed for admittance.

Kirk accepted the bundle, dismissed the man, and set about examining all the camouflage he would have on the strange world below. Sciences had assured him that, with a few minor changes, he, Spock, and Char Delminnen would be indistinguishable from the "Gypsies" they would soon move among.

The clothes were unremarkable, that being remarkable in itself. To look closely at them one would have guessed that they had been produced on a primitive hand loom instead of in the bowels of a matrix synthesizer. Kirk tried on the boots, the simple long pants and loose upper garment, the fur vest, and he finished by closely inspecting the carefully "aged" necklace with its concealed universal translator. The matching earpiece would appear to an uncertain observer as nothing more than a minor deformity—nothing sufficient to arouse anyone's interest.

Local currency was concealed in a sort of pouch-belt and consisted of a collection of small, heavy metal squares. Fortunately, the native coins were dull and poorly stamped. There were limits even to the *Enterprise*'s ultra-high-powered sensors.

Another buzz sounded insistently at the door.

"Come," Kirk said, for the door's benefit as much as that of his visitor. Responding to his verbal command, the single wedge slid aside.

Kirk examined himself in his mirror and turned to greet McCoy. "Well, Bones, do I look like a native?"

"You look like a fool," McCoy shot back tautly, "which I suppose is appropriate, since you're going on a fool's errand."

Kirk didn't reply, but waited for the doctor to finish.

"You don't mean to go through with this, Jim. This isn't a game being played with plastic pieces on some rec-room board. Kumara wants only two things out of this—Char Delminnen alive and you dead." He looked across at his friend, expression and voice straining for comprehension. "How can you possibly trust that—that—his very concepts of right and wrong are alien to ours!"

"Bones," Kirk began softly, "I knew Kumara when both of us were green, unspaced cadets. I know that was a long time ago, but from what I've seen these past days, he hasn't changed, and I don't think I have. He might steal you blind at the first opportunity, stab you in the back if he thought he could get away with it, lie, cheat—anything for an advantage."

McCoy was nodding knowingly. "Sounds like a Klingon gentleman all right."

"But he won't go back on that oath. He'll abide because he set the guidelines, Bones, not me. Yes, he'd do all those other things, given the chance, but he won't go back on that oath. And you're right—that *is* alien to us." Carefully he smoothed the pouch-belt around his waist, so that no tempting bulges would show.

"Besides, there's no way he could go back on his word after we've exchanged *nadas*."

McCoy momentarily forget his anger in puzzlement. "Exchange *nadas?* Didn't that have something to do with the hostage exchange you two were talking about?"

"That's right," confirmed the captain. "Another alien tradition, and another of the very few agreements binding on a Klingon. I hope you'll be comfortable during your visit to the *Klathas,* Bones."

It took much less than a minute for McCoy to digest the import of that statement. *"Me? I'm going to the Klathas?* But why me, Jim?"

"Because you're our resident servant and high priest of *Nada,* the Klingon god-patron of medicine. There have been reports of Klingons entering a hospital on board ship or on-planet and massacring the patients . . . but they have never touched a physician. It's part of their warrior-tainted cultural pattern. Your status on the *Klathas* will be that of a saint, Bones."

"Saint to a bunch of Klingons—I can't think of a less welcome honor."

"You'd better be grateful for it. It guarantees your immunity . . . and for that reason you're the only one I can trust the Klingons *not* to massacre if the contest goes against them. Naturally, while you're on board the *Klathas,* your Klingon counterpart will be here on the *Enterprise.*"

"But it's all unnecessary, Jim," McCoy objected one last time. "Kumara's set the whole thing up. He's called the rules, the place, everything. And another thing . . . How can you risk something as potentially dangerous as the Delminnen device on a two-man expedition?"

Kirk sighed. "I told you, Bones, it's our best chance for rescuing Van Delminnen." He started for the door.

McCoy put a restraining hand on his shoulder, still angry and still unconvinced. When he spoke again, his tone was low and almost accusing.

"Blast it, Jim, are you sure you're going through with this because you believe that—or because you're as vain about your ability to outmaneuver Kumara on a strange world as he thinks you are?"

Kirk glared at the doctor, and for a long moment what passed between them was as eloquent as it was unspoken. Finally: "You think Kumara's appealing to my vanity, then?"

"Is he, Jim?"

"I . . . I don't know. Maybe he is, Bones. Maybe he has already outmaneuvered me before the game's even started. But I do know this . . ." His voice rose.

"Besides keeping the weapon from the Klingons, there's also Char Delminnen to think of. It's our duty to save her brother, because he's a Federation citizen, because he's a human being. If I pass up a chance to do that to protect my own neck, Bones, then my commission's worthless.

"In addition, I'm going crazy waiting around while our engineering section races theirs to see who can fix their engines first. Don't you think Kumara's nervous? He's so nervous, *he's* the one who's proposed something to resolve part of our problem, given us the chance to do something besides sit around and wait for our fingernails to dissolve in our mouths.

"By all that's worth salvaging in this bizarre galaxy, Bones, I'm going to make the most of that opportunity."

Neither man moved until McCoy seemed to slump in on himself a little. He looked away. "All right. If I can't talk you out of it, at least I can accompany you to the transporter room."

"Sure you don't want to take anything with you, Bones," Kirk wondered, "to make your visit on the *Klathas* more bearable?"

"The only thing that could do that would be a Class Four phaser," the doctor grunted, "suitable for performing large-scale surgery on massed Klingon bodies. Let's go . . ."

X

"Captain's log, supplemental," Kirk recited, addressing the wall intercom in the Transporter Room. It was keyed by verbal command to the ship's log.

"Char Delminnen, Mr. Spock, and myself are preparing to beam down to the wandering world we have named Gypsy to commence a contest with our Klingon counterparts. We hope this contest will favorably resolve the stalemate in which we presently find ourselves with regard to her brother and the Imperial cruiser *Klathas.*

"In consequence of this, an exchange of ships' chief physicians has been effected, thus forcing a solemn bind upon the Klingons not to deviate from the rules set down for the competition ... with appropriate sensors and scanners also monitoring the terms of the contest.

"Doctor McCoy is now aboard the *Klathas,* and his Klingon doppelgänger, Surgeon-in-Battle Kattrun dek Prenn, has arrived aboard the *Enterprise.*" He paused for a second, finally adding, "I only hope that my evaluation of the incipient action turns out to be more accurate than Dr. McCoy's."

The entry ended, Kirk turned and walked past the transporter console to join a waiting Spock and Char Delminnen in the activated alcove. Briefly he noted the disposition of their native garb, the quality and detail of their facial makeup, and found everything satisfactory, if not visually pleasing.

"Ready, Mr. Spock?"

"Quite ready, Captain." He rubbed at the thick cap pulled low on his head. "Though this wig and attendant headgear are more than a little irritating."

"You'll get used to them, Spock. They're necessary—our Gypsies don't have acute hearing organs."

146

"An unfortunate evolutionary defect," the first officer commented drily.

Kirk smiled, then turned a more solemn, appraising gaze on the stiff figure at his right. "And you, Ms. Delminnen, are you sure you want to go through with this? Our success hinges on you, you know. I can't order you to participate."

Her reply was impatient. "I've already consented to it, Captain, as has my brother. The sooner we stop brooding about possible consequences and get on with it, the sooner Van and I will be reunited. Isn't that right?"

"That is very right." Convinced that the slight, hypertense woman would be an asset rather than a burden, Kirk turned to face back into the room. After a quick check of the chronometer disguised as a ring, he said pleasantly, "Energize when ready, Mr. Scott."

"Aye, Captain."

The chief engineer adjusted the necessary instrumentation, and in a moment the ship's population decreased by a three. At the same time, two beings of differing temperament and physical makeup lay in unfamiliar surroundings and began counting the minutes. There were a great many to pass until the end of three days, and none could say whether Dr. Leonard McCoy or SIB Kattrun dek Prenn counted harder . . .

A good deal of planning and examination of longrange sensor reports had gone into determining exactly where the party from the *Enterprise* should set down. Ideally, the place should offer temporary concealment without being too isolated, and without immediately exposing the strangers to the new world—or the new world to the strangers—before either had a chance to be acclimated.

So the three ministers in mufti materialized in the middle of a deserted alleyway. Faint people noises could be heard nearby, just loud enough for all three to properly adjust their necklace translators.

Even more than the damp alleyway with its claustrophobic high stone walls, even more than the always

mind-tingling sound of a new tongue, Kirk was drawn
to the sky overhead. The light was dimmer than was
usual on Earth, but more spectacular than the meteor-
ologists had predicted.

No one color dominated a sky that was aflame with
auroral blaze: Reds, greens, blues and golds and violent purple shifted and writhed in an atmosphere of
perpetual excitation. Whenever a particularly brilliant
display occurred, they would acquire a new phenomenon—a shadow. And the shadows changed constantly,
according to the varying intensity of the sky. To look
at one's own shadow was to be subject to a strobo-
scopic display of peculiarly personal dimensions.

A final check insured that no one had observed their
unorthodox method of arrival. "Everyone all right?"
Kirk whispered. His words sounded strange and tickled
his brain, voiced as they were through the translator in
the local tongue and then retranslated back through the
tiny device implanted in his left ear.

"Quite, Captain . . . ," "Yes, Captain . . . ," came the
replies.

"Okay, our first step is to obtain some local weapons.
I don't expect Kumara to waste any time in local sight-
seeing, so we'd better not either." He turned to face the
open end of the alley. "If Scotty dropped us where the
cartographers indicated he should, we ought to be next
to a fair-sized marketplace."

The group moved cautiously down the alleyway and
out into a strange new world of noise and movement
and color. The alley fronted on an extensive bazaar.
One old woman saw them emerge from the alley. If
she found it extraordinary, she chose not to publicize
the discovery. Kirk already suspected from the sociologists' preliminary reports that this was a world where
one minded one's own business.

They began to stroll down the long lanes between
stalls. The bazaar was a weird combination of old
Earth Arabian and medieval Edoan.

One thing that was never in doubt from the moment
they appeared was the efficacy of their disguises. They
were immediately besieged by hawkers and vendors

offering wares and goods and services as colorful as
they were enigmatic. There were many offered which
even Spock could make no sense of, and others which
seemed to conflict with laws natural and otherwise.

Their objectives now were too practical to be
disguised by alien rhetoric, however. Kirk adopted
what he hoped was just the right degree of imperious
indifference, ignoring bargains and luxuries alike.

"Something about this all strikes me as very strange,
Captain," Spock commented, his gaze moving from one
stall to the next.

"That's hardly surprising, Mr. Spock," replied Kirk,
fending off a proffered armload of aromatic meat.
"This whole world is very strange, from its very existence on down."

"Captain Kirk." He turned his attention to the booth
Char Delminnen was pointing at.

It was a tightly sealed, smallish shop, its narrow
tables replete with lethal-looking medieval-style weaponry, some faintly familiar, some less so. None was
beyond utilization by the new arrivals. There are only
so many ways to change the appearance of metal designed to penetrate another person without impairing
its efficiency.

Hands clasped over a well-cultivated paunch, the
proprietor stood staring pensively at the entrance to his
stall.

Kirk said, "Excuse me, we need to buy some
weapons." The translator, bearing in mind Kirk's assumed social station on this world, translated it as:

"Bestir thyself, o lazy one! We would purchase arms
from your pitiful stock."

The stall owner started and nearly fell over his own
legs in his haste to get to his feet. His eyes glittered
nearly as much as the false jewels in Kirk's necklace.

"Ten thousand genuflections, noble sir! The gods'
blessings on you and your offspring, may they be many.
You desire weapons? Rest content you have come to
the finest armory in the city. My most magnificent
steels and swords, knives and daggers, are un-
matched—and available especially to you, my lords

and lady, at prices so modest as to make one blush the color of her cheeks. Were you to search a thousand years through a hundred—"

"Enough, grandfather of loquacity! You have convinced us," Kirk declared, the translator once again having embellished his simple reply. He made a pretense of inspecting the stock. "We shall require two swords of your best metal and temper—sabers, not rapiers. And two dirks, short and tough enough to penetrate leather without turning." He hesitated. "And your most delicately honed stiletto for the lady."

Char Delminnen eyed him with satisfaction.

The owner was bowing and abasing himself to the point of embarrassing both Kirk and Spock, though it was more to conceal the mercenary gleam in his eyes than to honor his customers.

"At once, noble lords! You shall have the finest only. I do not keep the very best here exposed to the sky, and to thieves. Pray grant me a moment." Still bowing obsequiously, he backed into the depths of the stall.

Spock's attention had remained focused on the constantly moving, surrounding crowd. The first officer had been quite content to leave the purchasing to Kirk, who now turned to him, whispering.

"Any sign of Kumara or anyone who might be his accompanying officer?"

Spock shook his head. "If they are in our immediate vicinity, Captain, they are too well disguised for me to discover. I think we are still reasonably safe. Even at a fast run, it is still a fair distance to the other side of this town."

They separated as the owner, puffing heavily, appeared with the five weapons.

"As you requested, lords," he beamed, setting them out carefully on red velvet. "The apex of my humble craft. Notice the color in the metal, the superb honing!" He rambled on as Kirk and Spock hefted the swords, removing them from their matching scabbards. They made a few practice passes at each other with them, keeping the movements simple. Modern fencing might very well be an eye-catching anomaly here, and one thing they didn't desire was suspicious attention from the locals.

"I suppose they'll do," Kirk agreed, the words coming out in a bored and slightly petulant tone. He slid his saber into the scabbard, which attached easily to his pouch-belt. The thick, triangular dirks went through a belt loop on the opposite side from the sword. Char Delminnen found a secretive place for the narrow stiletto.

"I know you will be pleased, noble lords." His eyes narrowed and he leaned forward, lowering his voice. "It is plain you are not of Ghuncha Town, and are strangers here. Might I make so bold as to inquire—"

"As to the cost, which can be excessive for those who are too curious," Spock interrupted. His brows rose slightly at the way the translator interpreted his prosaic sentence.

"Certainly, yes," the proprietor babbled hastily. "I did not mean to pry, I did not . . . fifty *pahds,* noble sirs, will be more than sufficient."

"Since it is more than sufficient, it is doubtless more than we should pay," Kirk rumbled, reaching into the lining of his pouch-belt. "However, I have no time to haggle." He brought out a handful of brown metal squares. The shopkeeper's eyes nearly joined an unsold sword on the red velvet as Kirk counted out five of the largest squares and handed them to the man.

"Thank you, noble lords . . . blessings forever upon you," he called as they turned and began walking away. "Blessings a thousand times!"

"I'd trade a thousand blessings for a place to rest, Captain Kirk," Delminnen ventured many hours later. "Isn't it time to stop? There's no real night here, so we'll have to decide on our own."

"Innkeeping must be a round-the-clock business on Gypsy, Captain," Spock added. "We should have no difficulty in locating a busy one. Ms. Delminnen is correct. We must pace ourselves carefully or risk exhaustion at a crucial moment. The slightly greater gravity here does tend to weary one rapidly. I could use a meal myself."

"All right," Kirk agreed, wiping his forehead. The strain of trying to locate a Klingon under every curious face was beginning to tire him also. "It would be a good idea to establish some kind of local base of operations while we still have time for such things. Any sign of a likely prospect, Mr. Spock?"

The first officer was standing on tiptoe, staring ahead and slightly to their left. "I have already addressed myself to the problem, Captain. There appears to be an inn of some sort directly ahead of us."

A short walk brought them to the front of the establishment. They couldn't read the lettering on its front, but a quick, unobtrusive survey of the structure's exterior and the clientele carefully moving in and out through the oddly hinged multiple swinging—or was it folding—doors seemed to confirm Spock's initial appraisal. Furthermore, the appearance of those entering and leaving suggested a moderately high-class business.

That was enough for Kirk. They would have enough trouble remaining incognito without inviting conflict with the less savory elements of the native population. After watching the operation of the strange doors long enough to insure they wouldn't get pinched by them, he led Spock and Delminnen inside.

A system of mirrors and high windows admitted plenty of light. The interior wasn't much dimmer than the alley they had materialized in. To their left was a series of low tables at which some natives, mostly male, reclined while drinking and eating. To the right was a circular desk.

Between the two a long, paved walkway ran slightly above floor level until it met a branching stairway at the far end of the big room. This led up to a series of interior balconies before terminating in a large skylight three stories up.

A few patrons looked up, casually inspected the newcomers, and returned to their meals. Kirk noted the relative cleanliness of the place with satisfaction and moved to address the single opening in the high circular desk.

There was no one behind it. A small gong hung under a curved support to one side. Kirk lifted the tiny metal stick and hit the gong once, twice.

A tall, aged, cadaverous native appeared from an unsuspected doorway at the back of the concealed area. He wore an interesting arrangement of bloomers and overlapping vests, together with what would pass on Earth for a mournful expression. He looked more like a mortician than a concierge ... a fact which led Kirk to wonder about the perhaps deceptive peacefulness of the inn.

Nevertheless, they were here, and it was unlikely they would encounter any place better.

"What," the native asked tiredly, "do my lords require?"

"Food and lodging for this night and maybe several more. Your best room, on the second floor, one entrance only."

The native glanced at Char Delminnen, then back at Kirk. "One room, my lord, for the three of you?"

The translator turned Kirk's mild impatience into anger. "Yes, *one* room! Are you deaf—or do you wish to be? There must be sufficient individual bedding for all. You will see to it personally that suitable arrangements are made."

Either this native was made of stronger stuff than the weapons seller or he simply didn't care. "Whatever my lords require. I shall see to it."

Kirk turned as if to leave, then hesitated. "There is one more thing, innkeeper."

"My lord?"

"Have you yourself seen, or heard tell of, two men ... strangers like ourselves, with strong jaws and exceptional arrogance? They have a slightly foppish, tremendously arrogant younger man with them?" Kirk noticed Char Delminnen bridle at that description of her brother, but, if anything, the translators would only enlarge on his characterization of Van Delminnen's natural obstinacy.

The innkeeper paused thoughtfully. " 'Arrogance' is a strange word to use in identifying a man, my lord. I am sorry, but I am not in any way familiar with the persons you describe."

"I see," replied a disappointed Kirk. "Should you hear tell of such a group, inform us at once." He jiggled his pouch-belt significantly, so that the native could hear the clink of currency within.

The innkeeper merely bowed politely. "I shall do so, my lords." He gestured at the double stairway at the far end of the room. "Stairway on your right, second floor, third door down." A peculiarly shaped key was handed over. "Rest well. The room is already prepared as you desire."

Kirk frowned momentarily but then, why shouldn't such a room be readily available? He took the key, and they started for the stairs.

It was fortunate that the natives directions had been so explicit, since the carved squiggles on each door meant nothing to any of them. Kirk tried the door and found it unlocked, and they entered.

The room was spacious but dim, despite the large window. Spock moved to inspect it. He noted with a mutter of gratification that it was a sheer drop to the street below, and that the building facing them had no window directly opposite. They would have nothing to worry about from that quarter.

From there he moved to the door. Fishing into his own pouch-belt, he produced a tiny, simple lock. It looked like a local native handicraft, but was far stronger and more subtle than any lock on this world. He began to install it on the door.

"Spock and I are going to make one last sweep of our immediate area," Kirk was explaining to the exhausted Char Delminnen, "to make certain Kumara and your brother aren't close at hand. You may as well get some rest in the meantime." He nodded toward the door. "The lock Mr. Spock is installing is coded to respond only to our three voices."

"I'd like to go with you, Captain, but . . . I am tired. All right, I'll wait for you here. Wake me when you return. Then I can keep a watch while you and Mr. Spock take some rest."

"Sounds good, Ms. Delminnen. We'll try not to be too long." He reached out to pat her reassuringly on the shoulder—and froze as she leaned forward, up . . . and kissed him.

"Ready, Captain?" a blank-faced Spock asked from the half-open doorway.

Kirk gazed back at her uncertainly, finding her expression more unreadable than that of any other woman he'd ever seen. Whether there was affection, or curiosity, or something utterly incomprehensible in her stare he couldn't say.

"Coming, Mr. Spock."

The incident wasn't mentioned, and Spock gave every indication of having consigned it to the part of his mind reserved for filing inexplicable human actions. Kirk knew Spock had forgotten nothing, but he was grateful for his first officer's efforts to give the appearance of having done so.

Gradually it slipped from his mind too as they moved about the shops and homes and stalls, questioning the natives with increasing ease and the assurance that, while they were undeniably strangers, no one suspected how strange they actually were.

The questioning process became an exercise in consistent futility. No matter how detailed, how graphic, they made their descriptions of Kumara and Van Delminnen, they were greeted with the same negative response.

"No, noble lords, I have seen no one fitting such a description . . ." "Pardon, noble sirs, never have we heard tell of men with eyes such as you claim . . ." "No, I have not heard of them, or set sight of them myself . . ." "I have not . . ." "No . . ." "Not I . . ." "Never . . ."

By the time they returned to the inn, Kirk was too tired to care if Kumara was in this section of the town, or still at the opposite end, or back on the *Klathas.*

"I'd feel a lot better," he told Spock as they started

up the stone stairway, "if I knew Kumara's intentions. That's more important than his location."

A scream sounded from upstairs. It was slightly muffled, but still audible enough for both men to know instantly it did not come from a native throat.

"I believe we are about to obtain a partial answer to both questions, Captain."

The transporter could have gotten them upstairs faster—but not much faster. Kirk had a hand out, reaching for the door handle, when it opened from within. He found himself face to face with a short, stocky native. This individual, whose countenance screamed "thug," had one arm wrapped tightly around a weakly struggling Char Delminnen.

They stared at each other in momentary paralysis. The native saw Spock standing behind Kirk, computed the odds, and let go of Delminnen. Turning, he made a run for the open window as fast as his bandy, muscular legs could carry him.

Kirk brushed past the dazed Delminnen and tackled the native just before he could reach the rope dangling outside the window. Both men crashed to the floor, and Kirk discovered that he was grappling with a python. Gravity-stressed muscles shoved him onto his back, and he saw the glint of light on metal as the native raised the knife.

A hand came down on the native's shoulder, fingers moved quickly and skillfully, and the native collapsed. Panting heavily from the exertion under the strong gravity, Kirk slid out from under the unconscious form and climbed to his feet. Another figure drew him over to the far bed.

Char Delminnen was sitting there, shivering noticeably but otherwise apparently in control of herself. Kirk moved to touch her, hesitated, and drew back.

"He came in through the window?"

She nodded weakly.

"The rope is suspended from the roof, Captain," Spock reported. Holding on to the sill with one hand, he was leaning out over the street and peering upward. Now he came back inside and closed the window behind him. "I apologize, Ms. Delminnen. I was negligent in my analysis of this room's defensive potential. At the time it did not occur to me that one could as easily come down to this room as up to it. Curious oversight."

"Forget it, Spock," ordered Kirk. "I didn't think of it either. We're not used to acting like cat-burglars."

" 'Cat-burglars,' Captain? The reference—"

"Has nothing to do with stealing cats," Kirk hastened to explain. That brought a hesitant grin from Char Delminnen. She stopped shaking and gestured.

"I think my visitor is coming around, Captain."

Indeed, the native was emitting bubbling sounds indicative of rising consciousness. Spock helped him to his feet and steadied the man's staggers with one hand on his shoulder and the other holding an arm tightly behind his back.

The native looked fearfully from Char Delminnen to Kirk. He tried to break free ... but only once. Then his gaze dropped to the wooden floor, and he muttered sullenly, "What will you do to me ... noble lords." The last was uttered in a fashion clearly indicating that their nobility was in considerable question.

"Nothing ... if you answer a few questions," Kirk told him honestly. "Who sent you to kidnap the woman?"

The native remained silent. Spock moved his fingers on the man's shoulder in a certain way, and the man winced.

"Was it a tall man," Kirk continued evenly, "with very small pupils and dry-looking skin? Who moved quickly and with sharp gestures?"

The native's face twisted bizarrely as Spock applied further pressure. Finally: "Yes, yes ... now let me go, sirs!" As Spock's hand relaxed, so did the native's expression. "I'll tell you what you wish."

The first officer let go and took a couple of quick steps back, remaining between the native and the now closed window. Sighing in a very humanlike fashion, the native rubbed his neck and shook his freed arm to get the blood (or whatever served for bodily fluid here) moving again.

"Where did you meet this man?" Kirk continued.

"At the Inn of the Six Rains. He offered me three hundred *pahds* if I would bring him a woman he described to me." The native indicated the attentive Delminnen. "That woman."

"Was he alone?"

"No." The native looked thoughtful. "There were two other lords with him. One was very much like the first, but the third was different. He was smaller and quiet . . . in fact, he said nothing while I was present."

"Under orders from Kumara, no doubt, Captain," commented Spock.

"This other lord," Char Delminnen broke in, "who did not speak. Did he look well to you?"

The native eyed her curiously. "As well as the others . . . though I confess I paid little notice to him. It was the largest of the three lords I was concerned with."

"The one who offered you the money," Kirk declared pointedly. "This lord—he told you where to find the woman?"

"No."

Kirk relaxed considerably at that. That meant Kumara was probably not waiting for them downstairs, or rigging the stairway or preparing similar deviltry nearby.

"I found her myself, from the information the lord gave to me . . . gave to all of us."

"All of you?" Spock echoed. "There are more than one?"

"Aye. There were many present to hear the lord's offer."

"Why are you telling us this?"

The native made an indecipherable gesture. "Why should I help some other *cajjy* get rich?"

"It sounds like the sort of thing Kumara would do," mused Kirk sardonically. "Find himself a nice, peaceful room in a comfortable inn near his beam-down point, and then hire half the small-time cutthroats in town to do his dirty work for him, so he doesn't have to risk his own precious skin. Kumara's an atypical Klingon, Spock, but he's still a Klingon."

"I had not intended to dispute that, Captain," the first officer essayed easily. "I do wish to point out a significant new fact, however."

"What? What new fact, Spock?"

"Captain, we now have a distinct advantage. Kumara is ignorant as to our whereabouts, but we now know where he is based."

They exchanged glances. While they do so, the native showed that his body was more alert than his expression. He darted around a not-quite-fast-enough Spock, dove for the rope through the closed window, and missed.

All three rushed to the window. No crowd gathered below to inspect the body. On the contrary, there was a distinct absence of curiosity on the part of the populace.

"One native dead . . . one too many." Kirk looked over at his friend and second-in-command. "I think it's time we paid a visit to the Inn of the Six Rains, Mr. Spock."

"I agree, Captain."

They turned to leave. Char Delminnen was waiting by the door. She eyed Kirk expectantly.

"I can't leave you here and risk having another of Kumara's hired thugs finding you. Do you think you're up to coming with us, or should we hunt for another inn and wait a while longer?"

By way of answering she showed the stiletto, which her attacker had given her no opportunity to use, then slipped it back inside her blouse.

"Let's find my brother, Captain Kirk."

This time, she gave *his* shoulder a reassuring squeeze.

For a worried moment, Kirk was concerned that they might get no closer to the Inn of the Six Rains than the front door of their own inn. The dour manager was waiting for them by his enclosed moat of a desk, with two towering locals. The newcomers wore identical clothing. Kirk didn't think it was because they were relatives; he had been on enough worlds to recognize a uniform when he saw one.

"Captain," Spock whispered as the innkeeper gestured to them, "we could use the rope outside our room, ascend to the roof . . ."

"Easy, Spock. Surely other residents heard the scream. They can testify in our favor."

"There is trouble, my lords," the innkeeper explained sorrowfully.

"I can explain," Kirk began, addressing himself to the two giants instead of the speaker. "We had no intention of killing—"

The giant on the left interrupted. "Our concern is not with your intentions, or the question of killings, noble lord. But it is evident you are strangers here." He indicated the innkeeper, who looked embarrassed. "There is the matter of a shattered window."

It took a minute for the giant's words to penetrate. Once they had, Kirk settled the matter quickly. Spock chided him later for risking his cover by sinfully overpaying, but Kirk paid his first officer little heed. He was too glad to be free of local justice.

One thing was certain: They had encountered an ideal world on which to engage in Kumara's contest.

Local in-town transportation was nonexistent, they discovered the next day, but they had no difficulty in locating the Inn of the Six Rains once they had crossed the town's center. It seemed that everyone knew everything about the town, a consequence of having to walk everywhere.

The inn itself was nearly a duplicate of the one they had left, even to the fortresslike innkeeper's desk and the dining area opposite it. It had the same raised walkway in between, leading this time to a single stairway at its end. They did have the advantage of two things their old inn did not: booths and a noisy crowd.

Kirk found the atmosphere much more saloonlike than that of their own abode. Drinking was going on in earnest around them, and the air was filled with short, intriguing native laughter, shouting, and pungent smoke.

The innkeeper had assured the gentlemen that the three they searched for were indeed domiciled there. No, they were away at present. Perhaps they would return soon, to greet their friends from the country. In the meantime, why not sit and have good drink and pass tall stories around?

Kirk glanced across the busy tables at the innkeeper's station. He had watched the native carefully when they'd inquired after Kumara. Neither he nor Spock could detect any uncertainty at their questions, any sign of nervousness. The native had acted open instead of devious, and there was little they could do to test him further without arousing suspicions that seemed not to exist.

The three of them sat deep in a high-backed booth, playing at drinking thick wooden mugs of native brew while they carefully scrutinized the swinging doorway.

"Do you really think they'll return here, Captain Kirk?" Char Delminnen wondered uncertainly. Kirk touched the frothy mug to his lips and let a little slide down his throat. It was heady stuff, thick and spicy.

"They've no reason not to. That unfortunate native whose abduction we spoiled indicated that all of Kumara's hirelings are working alone. In fact, he exhibited a downright distaste for working with anyone else. So there's no way for Kumara to know that we've discovered his hiding place."

"That is a certainty, Captain," said Spock with conviction, gesturing toward the entrance.

Three figures came through the swinging doors leading into the inn from the street. Kirk had to blink, so thorough was the Klingon facial makeup. Nevertheless, he could recognize Kumara in the lead, followed by a disgusted-looking Van Delminnen, with another Klingon bringing up the rear of the little party.

Kirk had visions of watching them head straight up to their room, waiting until the Klingons were asleep, then stealing quietly upstairs to knock out any local guards and make off with Delminnen. This fantasy lasted until Char Delminnen jumped up and let out a joyful "Van—it's me, Van!"

About the only thing Kirk could salvage now was the memory of the startled surprise that appeared on Kumara's face.

"Come on, Spock!" Drawing their swords, they rushed toward Kumara.

Kirk engaged the Klingon commander, while Spock took on his assistant. It had been some time since he had worked with a saber, but certain things, once learned, are never forgotten. Not by the mind, and not by the body.

So while Kumara pressed him desperately hard at first, Kirk found himself gaining strength and confidence with each successful parry, each near cut. Char and Van Delminnen were clasping each other happily, chatting away as though neither one's fate and perhaps life was hanging in the balance.

The destruction engendered by the battle, which the other patrons were watching with stoic silence, was enough to bring a pleading, agonized innkeeper out from behind his desk.

"My lords ... Please, I beg you, my lords! Take your quarrels out in the street. Have pity on me, pity my house, my lords!"

Otherwise occupied, the four combatants utterly ignored him.

Finally the innkeeper turned and whispered something to a solemn little boy, who nodded in comprehension and rushed out. That left the florid proprietor standing before his disintegrating dining area, watching the battle, tight-lipped and silent.

"How—did you find us—Jim?" Kumara wondered, his wrist twisting and turning steadily, precisely.

Kirk caught an overhead blow on the flat of his blade, causing it to slide off harmlessly to his left, and countered with a cut of his own to the waist. He spaced his reply carefully between breaths.

"You should—hire a better class—of assassin, Kumara. The one who—found us—was willing to talk.

Money never inspires—much in the way—of loyalty. Pity for you."

"A pity—for you, Jim," countered the Klingon commander, his own sword making half circles in the air. "For now, much—as I dislike the thought—I am compelled—to kill you."

He turned the blade and lunged with the point, forcing Kirk backward.

Spock was pressing his opponent much more seriously. That engagement had begun with the other attacking furiously, wildly, drunk with self-confidence. Spock had blocked, retreated, parried every cut and thrust.

Gradually confidence gave way to rage, while Spock continued methodically to defend himself, content to let his opponent wear himself out—which was precisely what was happening. Now it was the *Enterprise*'s first officer who was pressing the attack, with equal precision, never giving his increasingly desperate counterpart a chance to rest.

An especially hard blow from his saber sent his assailant reeling. Panic showed in the Klingon's face. He backed, parrying wildly. Spock followed close—then suddenly his feet were gone from under him. He had slipped in a pool of stagnant drink, and abruptly found himself flat on his back.

Smiling triumphantly, his opponent jumped forward, his sword swinging high over his shoulder, ready to chop down heavily and slice flesh from bone.

Spock flipped his saber in his hand, caught it by the flat of the blade, and threw. The talkative armorer's claims had not been understated, and that possibly saved Spock's life.

The saber struck bone, but instead of snapping, it slid off. Its momentum carried it on through, its point coming out the back of the Klingon's shirt. A surprised, puzzled expression came over his face. His arm came down, and the sword flew from his hand. Spock was able to dodge—but not completely. The blade struck his forehead at an angle.

A hand came up, and then, blood welling from the wound, Spock fell back unconscious.

The Klingon officer's gaze turned slowly, slowly downward. It settled on the hurtful thing which penetrated him from front to back. Then his eyes closed, and he toppled onto a deserted table.

All the while, the crowd watched silently.

Kirk didn't see what had happened to Spock. He had no time. Kumara lunged again, forcing the captain back a little farther, and then made a peculiar thrust with his sword that no human could have duplicated. His blade came under Kirk's at the pommel, shoved and twisted—and Kirk's saber flew halfway across the room.

Grinning, Kumara lunged again, as Kirk grabbed a chair and swept it up before him desperately. The Klingon commander's sword pierced the wood and snapped cleanly in half as Kirk continued his swing with the chair.

Cursing, Kumara pulled and threw his knife, which Kirk caught on the chair's backswing. The captain threw the chair at Kumara, drew his own dirk, and followed the projectile. Kumara's hand came up frantically to catch Kirk's wrist, and then the two men were tumbling over and over each other through the sticky, food-filled gaps between the tables.

Both arms swung out and around to strike one unyielding chair leg. Kirk's wrist suddenly became numb, and the knife flew five meters. The combatants continued to roll about, arms and legs thrashing violently.

None of the onlookers attempted to interfere. They continued to watch dispassionately as the two strangers were reduced to swinging weakly at each other, each barely able to fend off the attacks of the other.

"Con—cede." Kumara gasped in pain, his head bobbing loose on his neck as though springs and not ligaments kept it joined to his head.

Kirk shook his head slowly, lacking the strength for a verbal reply—and even that action nearly caused him to collapse.

Several giants entered the room, ducking their heads to pass through the entrance. The largest looked at the room, his gaze traveling slowly from left to right to take in the two Delminnens, now also watching the battle on the floor, the two barely erect combatants weaving in its center, the dead one on the floor, and the injured one lying nearby.

He shook his head slowly from side to side, and the gesture was echoed by many in the silent crowd.

XI

A hand moved lazily, drawing delicate designs in the dust. Kumara considered what he had wrought, then obliterated it with a wave of his palm. His sole real complaint about the cell was that there was nothing to lean against save the chill stone walls.

Otherwise, it was the absence of certain devices which made it far more pleasurable a place to idle than its Klingon counterpart. He forced himself to sit away from the wall as he looked across the straw-and-dirt floor at his companions.

Kirk gazed back quietly. Several hours ago he and Kumara had tried their best to kill each other. Now they sat unbelligerently in the same room, in the same fix, and wished devoutly that their captors would put off doing anything until the contest's time limit had elapsed, at which time their respective transporters would pull them back to the safety of the two cruisers.

If not, Kirk mused, Scotty was liable to beam several corpses aboard the *Enterprise*. One area which the sociologists had not researched was Gypsian penology.

His eyes left Kumara and traveled around the windowless cell. Spock was busy rewinding the bandage around his forehead. The Delminnens sat off in a corner by themselves, still engrossed in each other and no doubt cursing Kirk, Kumara, and all the others who'd meddled in their lives.

"I must compliment you, Mr. Spock," Kumara said into the low drone formed by the Delminnens. "I happened to observe you at the moment when you dispatched Lieutenant Kritt. That was an admirable bit of quick thinking and reaction, which Kritt ought to have anticipated." The commander's mouth twisted into an unreadable expression. "Kritt always was an overconfident fool."

166

"It was," Spock replied, his voice absolutely flat, "the only logical thing left to do. I had hoped merely to disarm him, not to kill."

"I might have supposed you would say something like that," Kumara declared. Spock did not reply, so the commander turned his gaze heavenward.

"Ah, Gods, what a way for a Klingon officer to die. Here I sit, helpless among my enemies—me, the commander of one of the most powerful instruments in the galaxy. Doomed I am to die via some no doubt unimaginative method concocted by a council of superstitious barbarians."

"Quite a performance, Kumara," Kirk commented when the commander's plaint had ended, "but you always did make a specialty of substituting show for substance. I'm surprised at your resignation. If we can stall things for another day and a half, or if our captors remain inactive, our transporters will pluck us safe and free. And remember, it was your idea that we descend without modern weapons."

"Advanced weaponry could have stimulated latent cowardice," Kumara shot back.

Kirk started to move toward the Klingon, but Spock reached out to restrain him. "Easy, Captain, there is nothing to be gained by fighting now. The opportunity to escape may eventually present itself . . . though I am not optimistic." He looked up. "This cell is well designed with an eye toward preventing any such occurrence." His gaze dropped to Kumara. "Even if it was constructed by mere superstitious barbarians, who are advanced enough to confiscate our communicators."

The Klingon commander had no comment.

"Suppose we did escape?" Kirk turned to look over at Char Delminnen, as did Kumara. "Wouldn't you two have to begin again with Van and me?" There was bitterness in her voice.

Surprisingly, it was Kumara who replied. "Young female, if allowing you and your sibling to depart peacefully homeward would do anything to alleviate our present difficulties, I would be the first to see you safely on your way. Unfortunately, I fear that circumstances have long since been in control of all our destinies, so that, while possibly accurate, your accusations will never be put to the test. I suspect that we are all to be tried together—if the concept of a trial exists on this orphaned world."

"Whatever they have planned for us can't be any worse than Klingon justice," commented Kirk with a vicious smile. Now it was an angry Kumara's turn to start forward.

Spock forestalled further hostilities by assuming a pose of attention and announcing, "Not now, gentlemen. Several people are approaching."

All five hurried to scramble to their feet. A small party of armed men appeared outside their cell. Among them Kirk recognized the jailer, who had brought them food and water, and the leader of the group of giants that had brought them here from the Inn of the Six Rains.

The jailer worked on the crude (but efficient) lock while the rest of the party warily eyed those on the other side of the cementwork.

"You are to be given the privilege of pleading your case before the Justice Council. Come along . . . and mind your words and manner. The Council is not to be trifled with."

Guarded beyond any chance of making a run, they were convoyed up stairs, down corridors, and around bends. The room they finally arrived in was modest in size and decor. At one end was a high bench with a single high podium at its center. This was backed by five empty seats. Auroral blaze lit the room, shafting down through a high-domed glass ceiling.

Several tiered benches formed concentric semicircles at the opposite end of the room, and scattered, somewhat bored natives occupied these. They seemed to perk up a little when the captives entered, though.

Kirk and the others were conducted to a long padded bench which faced the higher bench and podium at the near end of the room. Their guards directed them to sit, then moved to join other guards at the two doors.

A single short, elderly native clad in dress of the utmost simplicity appeared. The grating, off-key tune he played was as weird and unnerving as the trumpetlike instrument he performed it on. At this signal, a hidden door opened behind the podium and five natives—two men and three women—appeared. They assumed the five seats before the captives. Kirk noted with interest that they were also clad in plain dress, including the old man who took the podium seat. There was nothing to distinguish their office, nothing to differentiate them from the poorest beggar in the streets. Cleanliness, perhaps, but then, even the beggars Kirk had seen in the marketplace had been fairly clean.

They were all solemn and stern-faced, however. "Self-righteous-looking bunch, aren't they?" Kirk found himself whispering to a frozen Kumara.

The Klingon commander let out a derisive snort. "Trial indeed! I will sell you my chance of being found innocent for two *pahds* and a good killing joke."

Spock tapped Kirk on the arm and gestured to the far door at a fat, smug-looking native. "There's the local who called for official help."

Kirk studied the man, who smiled back at him strangely.

"Looks content, doesn't he?" Kirk commented finally, though he was still uncertain of the other's expression. What was behind that peculiar grin? He chalked it up to the simple fact that the innkeeper was by the door while he, Spock, and the others were relative parsecs from that freedom.

Kirk turned his attention back to the judges, for such they had to be. They had all assumed their seats and proceeded to lapse into various postures of indifference. All were incredibly old. One, Kirk noted, was nearly asleep already. Another was deeply engrossed in inspecting her fingernails.

Only the occupant of the podium chair appeared reasonably alert. A portly, grave-visaged native, he took three handfuls of sand from a box on his left and ceremoniously transfered them to a box on his right, all while steadily muttering some whispered alien incantation.

The trial got under way when this formidable-looking individual followed the sand ritual by leaning forward and glaring down at them.

"Well?" he said gruffly.

"Well what?" countered Spock evenly. Kirk eyed his first officer uncertainly.

"How do you plead?" asked the judge irritably.

"I would like to know what we are expected to plead for," Spock continued. "To do that, we must know what we are accused of."

The judge looked further irritated. "Oh, very well, if you must." He peered down at something hidden from below. "You are all accused of disturbing the peace, letting blood on a forbidden day, destruction of private property, contributing to unnatural death, obfuscation of a legitimate business . . ."

While the list grew, Kumara leaned over and whispered worriedly to Kirk, "Did we do all that, Jim?"

"If he says so," Kirk murmured back, "I guess we did."

" . . . and being a public nuisance," the venerable praetor concluded eventually. He looked back down at them and coughed. "Have you anything to say in your own defense?"

That said, he leaned back, crossed his hands in front of him, and appeared to lapse into sleep.

There was a pause from below . . . and then Kumara was on his feet, gesticulating wildly for attention. "I can explain it all, Your Greatness!" Kirk stared at the commander open-mouthed.

"It is all so simple," Kumara said, talking very fast. "My companion and I were preparing to enter our lodging when, without cause or warning, these two ruffians beside me assaulted us." He took on a grieving tone. "Attacked us and murdered my best friend!"

The paralysis finally left Kirk, and he was practically inside Kumara's shirtfront. "Now just a *minute!*"

"Your pardon, sir," said Spock. The judge cocked an eye at the first officer, then looked back at Kirk and Kumara, who were ready to start in on each other again.

"You two sit down and behave yourselves. You, sir," he said to Spock, "may speak."

Kirk and Kumara resumed their seats as Spock rose. "This man and his companion had taken by force another man"—he indicated Van Delminnen—"whom we were trying to rescue, in order to return him to his sister, whom you see seated next to him. As the abductors were unwilling to return him peacefully, we were compelled to resort to force."

"That's a lie!" shouted Kumara, leaping to his feet again. "If *they* had merely turned the woman over to *us*, none of this would have happened."

"Is this true, sir?" the judge asked Spock.

"Your Greatness, it may be that the single death of the man I killed in self-defense could have been avoided, but in the long run many—"

"But it *could* have been avoided?" the judge persisted. "In fact, the entire fight could have been avoided?"

"Strictly from a logical point of view, yes," Spock, admitted looking rather unhappy, "but one must consider the long view, and when one does that it is immediately apparent that—"

"That's very interesting, thank you," the judge said, cutting the first officer off.

Kumara looked as though he had won a victory of sorts. "Besides, it is well known that all Vulcans are congenital liars," the commander added.

Kirk looked at his enemy in shock. "Kumara! Do you realize what you're saying?"

The judge looked interested. "And what, pray tell, is a Vulcan?"

Kumara pointed, his anger and frustration having driven him past all rationality now. "*That* is a Vulcan, your greatness! An alien in your midst, an interloper, a monster with a computer for a mind and a machine's sense of ethics! An insipid, unimaginative, soulless automation who—"

Spock bore the steady stream of insults and imprecations stolidly. The judge, looking bored, finally cut Kumara off in mid-insult.

"Your claim that you are innocent will be taken under advisement," he told him tiredly. He looked at Spock. "Do you, whatever or whoever you are, acknowledge the truth of any part of this person's claims?"

"Of course not," Spock said, looking straight at Kumara. The Klingon commander threw up his hands and sat down hard on the bench.

"Thank you, sirs." The judge yawned. "That ... that will do. I will now consult with my colleagues." He slid down from his chair and began poking and prodding the other ancients to wakefulness. Once active, all five retired behind the podium. Kirk could hear the tantalizing buzz of their conversation rise and fall, always just outside the range of decipherability.

"You fool!" Kumara whispered angrily at Spock. "Couldn't you see what I was attempting to do? With even one of us free, he might be able to hire help to rescue those reimprisoned!"

Spock's eyebrows rose alarmingly, though his voice remained unchanged. "And you said that *Vulcans* were congenital liars."

Kumara had a properly sarcastic retort prepared, but the reappearance of the five judges forestalled it. He turned as anxiously as the others while the ancients resumed their seats. All seemed almost awake now, as though it were necessary to bestir themselves at least for pronouncement of sentence.

"I see that your bickering has ceased," the high judge observed, with evident satisfaction. "That is well, as we have deliberated and reached a decision." He yawned again.

"Before you make your decision known, Your Greatness, I would like the answers to several questions. You can hardly deny them if you are prepared to execute or imprison us." Spock waited resolutely for a reply.

The high judge considered, and finally grumbled,

"Oh, if you must. But make them interesting, lest we lose interest quickly."

"I believe you will find them interesting enough," Spock declared. He began to pace back and forth beneath the high bench, asking his questions as he walked. Kirk and Kumara watched him with equal curiosity.

"Why is it," the *Enterprise*'s first officer wondered, "that, despite the large number of resting places, and a perpetual daylight that would seem to preclude any regular resting time, we have never seen a single one of your even appear drowsy? Why have we not seen a single live animal, despite an abundance of fresh-killed meat in the marketplace?

"Why the total absence of even simple vehicles, and the lack of interest in our battle to the death at the inn? Such a crowd would seem to be the type most interested in such conflicts, yet they uttered hardly a sound throughout the fighting.

"Then there is the very existence of this world, which defies so many natural laws. Despite this, we find ourselves confronted with a civilization and race that, excepting trivial differences, could be a duplicate of an earlier terrestrial or Klingon culture. That implies a coincidence of evolution under radically different conditions—a coincidence we have until now had no choice but to accept."

"Spock, what are you getting at?" Kirk asked.

His first officer turned to him, the conviction in his voice growing with each succeeding sentence. "Have the events of the past weeks not struck you as rushed, Captain? Do you accept the existence of the world you see around you here, regardless of the fact that our entire body of scientific knowledge declares it a flagrant impossibility?"

"Your first officer is mad, Captain Kirk," declared Kumara, watching Spock warily. "He denies the evidence of his own senses."

"Senses can be fooled," Spock went on, turning to the Klingon commander, "but a rational mind cannot. It has taken until now for the weight of successive incongruities to point out the greater one. I am beginning to believe my mind, not my eyes." He turned back to Kirk.

"Do you accept the existence of this world as you see it, Captain? Because I do not."

Kirk felt the hard wood of the bench beneath him, looked around and saw the eyes of judges, guards, innkeeper, and spectators on him, breathed deeply of the air, studied the iridescent sky through the glass dome, and replied, "Have I a choice, Mr. Spock?"

Spock sighed heavily. "Think, Captain. We have in the past few weeks encountered two near duplicates of Terran ecology and humanoid civilization. In both cases the natives could, with very slight alterations, pass for human, Vulcan, or Klingon with relative ease. Both the world of Arret, in the negative universe, and this wandering planet support such civilizations in heretofore unsuspected astronomical environments. A mere coincidence? It boggles the mind."

Spock turned to face the judges, and Kirk noted with surprise that all five were now wide awake, more attentive than they had appeared at any earlier time.

"Whatever the explanation, you must confess, Your Greatness, whoever you are, that these coincidences leave a great deal unexplained."

"I would say that is putting it mildly, Mr. Spock."

All eyes turned to the source of that voice. Kirk's thoughts turned upside down, as his whole universe had during the course of Spock's speech.

"Karla Five!"

The woman walking toward them from the near door was none other than their pied piper into the negative universe bridged by the Beta Niobe Nova.

"I don't," Kirk muttered plaintively, "understand."

"Nor do I, Captain, but I have suspected. The very unlikeliness of Arret and this world suggested a possible tie, though I am still ignorant as to what it might be."

"Never mind, Mr. Spock," Karla Five said reassuringly, "it was your willingness to voice what your mind suspected which has decided the trial in your favor.

You were beginning to disappoint us." She turned to the judge's bench.

"I believe the time has come to end the masquerade, colleagues." She waved her right arm slowly, expansively.

The courtroom vanished. So did the town. Kirk, Spock, and Kumara found themselves standing alone on a rolling, grassy plain which ran unbroken to every horizon.

Well, not exactly alone . . .

Kirk squinted and held his hands in front of his face to shield himself. Where the judges had sat moments before were now suspended five meter-wide globes of radiant energy, each glowing like a miniature sun. Another globe occupied the position held a moment before by Karla Five.

Perhaps the biggest surprize was the presence of the last two globes, which drifted and swirled about each other in the places occupied only seconds ago by Van and Char Delminnen.

Kirk felt sanity slipping away, like water down a drain, and screamed inside himself for something solid, something real, to hold on to. It was provided by his own mind, which could find no room for panic amid all the curiosity.

"Who . . . what are you?"

The energy thing that had been Karla Five expounded in a deep non-voice. "We are the Wanderers Who Play," the not-words elucidated. "We are Those Who Meddle. We are the ones who long ago—so long ago that your terminology is not great enough to encompass it—deserted our final corporeal bodies for the configurations of pure energy which you now see."

"You said you play," Kirk said, eyes tightly slitted against the wonderful glare. "What do you play at?"

"Existence," the second judge murmured.

"To what purpose?" This typical expression of practicality came, naturally, from Spock.

"Amusement and edification," explained the judge of judges. "At regular intervals we conduct a tour of various galaxies which remain of interest to us. This we do to record the progress and development of the local space-traversing dominants. In this case, yourselves, gentlemen. Our attention is magnified when several dominant forms expand far enough to come into conflict with one another.

"For reasons of convenience, and a certain amount of what you would term nostalgia, we have utilized this world as the vehicle for transporting us through space. It is our original home world. We are attached to it. And, while it serves no real purpose but one, that is sufficient to trouble taking it with us."

"That single purpose is information storage, gentlemen," continued the light that had been Karla Five. "We need a fair-sized solid for that. Our world serves us admirably. We have, of course, no need for the warmth and light which our exceptional atmosphere, as Mr. Spock calls it, provides.

"However, we still enjoy the presence of living things around us. We have the time and patience necessary to luxuriate in the contemplative thought patterns of growing plants."

"You have been undergoing a test," the judge of judges told them, "a test which is now concluded."

"The humanoid civilization?" Kirk asked, gesturing at the open expanse of prairie around them. "The city, its people . . . it was a laboratory experiment, in which we were guinea pigs?"

"Restrain your bitterness, Captain Kirk," said Karla Five. "We mean you neither ill nor good. Allow us this harmless academic pleasantry."

"Lieutenant Kritt didn't find it very harmless," Kumara muttered. Karla Five's reply was filled with reproof.

"That was of your own choice and doing, Commander Kumara. We did not interfere. We only studied. When you and Captain Kirk persisted in your futile battle at the inn instead of attempting to work out a peaceful settlement of your differences, we were most disappointed. Most."

"Terribly sorry," Kumara countered sarcastically. "The experimental animals offer their apologies. Perhaps you didn't bait the maze sufficiently to produce the reactions you wanted."

"Speaking of differences and bait and mazes," Kirk said, "what of that negative universe?"

"It did not exist, not in the form you believed you saw it in," Karla Five told him. "Even we cannot accomplish a passage into something which does not exist. It was created as the first part of your test, from a play theory one of us had generated."

"Mine," said the fifth judge, with a touch of pride. "It was rather a good theory. Pity it does not exist."

"Even if it did," Karla Five went on, "a less likely method of interdimensional travel than diving into a raging nova would be difficult to imagine.

"You accept too readily the evidence of your senses instead of your mind, Captain Kirk, Commander Kumara—even you, Mr. Spock. Think again on the people of Arret—would a race which appeared with all the knowledge it would ever have be able to exist, once its devolution was a known fact? No, it would go mad with the knowledge. Would an Arretian child be born in a grave, as a senile adult form, only to die within a living mother? For that matter, by what process would a new Arretian come into existence?

"I am surprised at you all for not seeing through that first fabrication. But then it was necessary to bring you together, to see if you would react more sensibly than you did apart. As you know, you have not."

Kirk looked over at Kumara, and found the commander staring back at him. "Negative universe—you too, Kumara?"

The commander nodded slowly. "A mere two *triaines* ago. We did not think we would survive. The negative world which aided us was a near duplicate of Klingon. In fact, its name was—"

"Nognilk," put in Spock.

"The very same," admitted the tired commander. "The inconsistencies ... Why did we not sense them before!"

"And the Delminnens?" Kirk asked.

Somehow the judge of judges managed to convey the

impression of indicating the two globes which swirled and darted about each other.

"These two Wanderers were given the task of playing at being human, at being the humans Delminnen. The message from your Starfleet base, Captain Kirk—and your Imperial Sector headquarters, Commander Kumara—was an artifice of ours, designed to bring you hastily to the system designed. We followed your foolishly primitive attempts to unite the human couple through violence with considerable sadness.

"In the end, it seemed that total destruction of one vessel or the other must result. Hence our appearance here at the crucial moment, to prevent that. It was we, Commander Kumara, who planted the suggestion of a contest in your mind."

Kumara looked shaken.

Spock broke in: "But the Delminnens are real people."

"So they are, Mr. Spock," admitted Karla Five. "They continue their hermitage on the far side of their moon from where you set down, quite unaware that anything out of the ordinary has taken place. Incidentally, they aré as harmless as your records indicated. Should you return to their system, you will find planets Eight and Nine orbiting their sun unchanged—their 'destruction' merely being another of our engineered illusions."

"World-maker or not," Kumara whispered to Kirk, "I'd hit it if I could be sure of contacting something."

"We must leave you now, gentlemen," Karla Five continued. "There are many among us who have profited from your actions of the past seconds—seconds only to us, of course, weeks to you. We are sorry at the laggard pace of your development."

"What do you intend to do with us?" Kirk asked hesitantly.

"You will all be returned to your respective ships and permitted to return home. But carry with you this warning, which we make most regretfully.

"If your races have not made substantial improvement over your present degree of maturity, or rather lack of it, by the time of our next visit to this portion of this galaxy, we will be compelled to regard you as degenerates incapable of proper development. Consequently, you will be eliminated from the cycle of advance.

"Good-bye, Commander Kumara." Karla Five glowed bluely, and the Klingon commander was gone.

"Back to his vessel, and McCoy to yours," the globe explained. "And now—"

"Wait!" Kirk shouted. "Why do you care? Why this concern with our development, this need for elaborate interference?"

There was a pause; then: "We strive constantly to upgrade the maturity of those races we encounter, Captain Kirk, in the faint hope that one day one or more of them will reach our own level. It is very lonely to exist at the apex of creation, for an apex is surrounded always only by emptiness."

"How much longer do we have . . . before you return again?" the captain asked hurriedly.

"Not long, I fear," confessed the judge of judges. "No more than another twelve of your millennia. Now go . . ."

And they were gone.

Sulu was studying standard readouts from the world below. He turned to inform Uhura of one especially interesting discovery—and nearly fell from his chair as the captain rematerialized in his. Uhura had started to turn at Sulu's call, only to pause and gasp as the science station was once again occupied by its usual tenant.

Although he stood between the two materializations, Dr. McCoy was too pleased to see both men return alive to be shocked. That would come later.

"Jim . . . Spock! How did I . . . How—what happened down there?"

Kirk felt the comforting solidity of the command chair. That, at least, was real . . . wasn't it? At least it was as real as the mystifying globe sitting alone in the viewscreen. Amazing how one could overlook the obvious when confronted by the impossible.

"Mr. Sulu?"

"Yes, sir?"

"What is the mass of the world below us?"

Sulu looked puzzled, while at Kirk's right McCoy was barely able to hold himself in check. "The mass, Captain? But we already measured—"

"Compute it again, Lieutenant."

Sulu proceeded to carry out the puzzling order, bent closer over his instrumentation, and finally looked back in total confusion.

"I don't understand it, sir. There's a new reading, but it's impossible."

"What is it?"

"According to the latest readings, the mass of Gypsy is only point six four that of Earth. But the gravity reading remains constant. That's impossible."

"Not this time, Mr. Sulu. The gravity is correct, and no doubt artificially enhanced. While the mass—"

"—is undoubtedly correct," Spock finished for him, "for a mobile filing cabinet of such size."

McCoy looked askance from one to the other. "Jim, what is all this . . . this talk of filing cabinets and artificial gravity? How did you get back here, anyway?"

"Twelve thousand years," Kirk murmured, not hearing.

"What . . . what's that?"

"Captain," Arex reported, "the *Klathas* is picking up speed. She's moving out of the area on impulse power."

Kirk moved to the intercom. "Engineering . . . This is the captain speaking. Scotty, are you there?"

"Aye, Captain."

"Do we have enough power to get under way?"

"Aye, but barely. I think we can manage warp-two, but not much more."

"It'll do. Thank you, Scotty." He clicked off, then turned back to face the helm once more. "Mr. Sulu, set course for Babel. I have a story that's going to interest Commodore April. It seems he and Sarah owe their unexpected rejuvenation to a dream . . . unless that's an illusion too."

"I think not, Captain," declared Spock thoughtfully. "It was the Aprils who pulled us through the first part of the Wanderers' test. Clearly they were impressed. The Aprils' new life strikes me as a realistic reward for . . . for a maze well run."

"Excuse me, sir," Sulu wondered, "but we have superior speed now. Aren't we going after the Klingons?"

"No, Mr. Sulu . . . and they are no longer concerned with us. Kumara has too much else to think about now."

"In heaven's name, Jim," an exasperated McCoy blurted out, "what happened? Why are we suddenly running from the *Klathas* . . . and it from us? And by the way, where's Char Delminnen?"

"Twelve thousand years," Kirk whispered again. Then, louder: "Home is where the heart is, Bones—if the mind concurs. Rest easy that the Delminnens are perfectly safe."

McCoy turned in frustration to Spock, who was busy as usual at his library computer console. "Spock, you tell me. What's Jim mumbling about? What does he mean?"

"What he means, Doctor, is that we had all best learn to be good little boys and girls or we're liable to get spanked."

McCoy, now unable even to voice his questions, gawked at the first officer. Spock turned casually to Kirk. "There is one more thing which worries me, Captain."

"What's that, Mr. Spock?"

"The negative universe of Arret was an illusion. The world of Gypsy was an illusion. Both were part of a test originated by the Wanderers. Yet we have only their word for their own existence . . . the word of illusion creators. What concerns me, Captain, is . . . might not the Wanderers be only part of some greater illusion, some greater test?

"For that matter, how much of our universe is real—and how much an illusion, created by forces unimaginable merely to test us?"

"Mr. Spock," murmured Uhura, "that almost sounds religious."

Spock started to reply, hesitated, and finally said, "It may be interpreted variously, Lieutenant Uhura, but recent experiences tend to make one pause before disregarding anything. What do you think, Captain?"

Kirk looked at the viewscreen, which showed the globe of Gypsy receding into a vast, star-speckled blackness. "I think, Mr. Spock, that we'd better make the best we can of this universe—it's the only illusion we've got, and it's not a bad one."

He leaned back in the command chair and prepared to record the final log entry to the strange episode, then paused, reflective.

Was all life lived only in an illusion, or was his reality someone else's fantasy? Finally, he shrugged and activated the log. The entry he was about to make, detailing the journey to Arret and the subsequent encounter with the Wanderers, would be real enough to him, would form a real record from which someone else would have to make the final judgments. He smiled.

Anyone who read those log entries couldn't possibly dismiss them as illusion . . .

THE COMPLETE STAR TREK LIBRARY
from
🅱🅱
BALLANTINE BOOKS

THE WORLD OF STAR TREK
David Gerrold
The Show • The Original Conception •
The Writers • The Stars • The Technicians •
The Fans • And LOTS More • With PHOTOS!

THE TROUBLE WITH TRIBBLES
David Gerrold
The complete story of a television script:
How it was written, filmed, and what happened
when it finally appeared on the air as an
episode of STAR TREK. LOTS OF PHOTOS.

THE MAKING OF STAR TREK
Stephen E. Whitfield & Gene Roddenberry
The book on how to write for TV! The entire
authentic history. Fully illustrated.

$1.95

▼ **Available at your local bookstore or mail the coupon below** ▼

BB 80/75